Charle

Which is the Winner?

Vol. 3

SALZWASSER
VERLAG

Charles Clarke

Which is the Winner?

Vol. 3

Reprint of the original, first published in 1864.

1st Edition 2022 | ISBN: 978-3-75259-556-7

Verlag (Publisher): Salzwasser Verlag GmbH, Zeilweg 44, 60439 Frankfurt, Deutschland
Vertretungsberechtigt (Authorized to represent): E. Roepke, Zeilweg 44, 60439 Frankfurt, Deutschland
Druck (Print): Books on Demand GmbH, In de Tarpen 42, 22848 Norderstedt, Deutschland

WHICH IS THE WINNER?

WHICH IS THE WINNER?

OR,

The First Gentleman of his Family.

By CHARLES CLARKE,

IN THREE VOLUMES.

Vol. III.

LONDON

1864.

CONTENTS OF VOL. III.

WHICH IS THE WINNER?

CHAPTER I.

A SLOW RECOVERY PREPARATORY TO FALLING AGAIN.

'Not very dangerous, except to those that are careless; but withal, he *blushed* as he spoke.'—*Pilgrim's Progress:* Bunyan.

'Percussion of the brain,' as the Sommerton groom called it, is an exceedingly unpleasant condition of life. Whatever it was that affected Lord Mentmore, he was carried, as we have seen, senseless into the house. A suite of rooms was immediately prepared for him; messengers were sent to Spring Vale, to apprise his late hosts, and to desire his valet to come over to Sommerton; and to Saxonby, to fetch Dr. Probewell, who made use of such hard language as to frighten the housekeeper and his lordship's valet exceedingly. 'Pupils dilated, stertorous breathing, absence of pulsation,' said the doctor. However, it was a great day for him; and the first earl that he had ever had the pleasure of prescribing for gave a dignity to his manner, and a consequence to his orders, when he returned home, which was more amusing to his neighbours than gratifying to his own household.

But when such a carcase as this is to be fed upon, it is considered the right thing to call in more vultures, lest the solitary provincial bird shall become too much swollen with fatness, or the body should fail of proper honours. So they sent off to the county town for an eminent surgeon, and to London for the earl's own physician. The last was a little bored by the journey, which he took in the night, to save time, and for which, at an early period of Mentmore's recovery, he received a cheque of seventy-five guineas. The infirmary surgeon and the country practitioner divided the rest of the booty pretty equally, the former receiving his in the more honourable way of fees, the latter in the more profitable one, of visits, bolus, draught, pills as before, *ad infinitum,* until about the third week, in spite of most energetic remonstrances, Lord Mentmore would go out riding, and was obstinately denied to his medical man.

'How do you feel to-day, Mentmore?' said young Bradfield, entering his room, towards the end of the first week, and sitting down in an armchair, opposite the sofa on which his friend was lying.

'Better, thanks to your kindness; rather dizzy and weak, but that will be all right in a day or two, I hope.'

Bradfield shook his head.

'Not quite so soon as that. Fellows don't lie insensible for about eight-and-forty hours to get all right in a day or two. However, I'm glad to see you as well as you are.'

'Have my letters been sent up from Spring Vale, Bradfield?'

'Yes; Sir Michael and Stafford Carrington brought them over yesterday, and wanted to see you, but you were asleep, and old Probewell—'

'Old Humbug wouldn't let them, I suppose.'

'I think he's right, for a day or two, I must confess.'

'Come, Bradfield, nonsense; I surely may see anyone to-day? I'm nearly as well as ever. Just look here,' and the impatient young nobleman essayed to walk, and nearly tumbled down, upsetting a small round table and a piece of china in his struggles to save himself.

'Now you're satisfied, Mentmore, I hope.'

'I'm satisfied I am not as strong as you are. I never was. But I cannot see why I should not see Carrington, if he calls.'

'Well! you shall see him; only behave discreetly. Not too long, nor too much talking. Are you tired now?'

'Not in the least.'

'Then tell me how it happened, for I've never heard.'

'The hounds were close to their fox, as I

thought, and being anxious for a kill, after so good a run, I was galloping as fast as I could go along the outside of the cover. I think Beneventum was a little leg weary—almost everything was beat—and he put his foot into a drain, or a rabbit-hole, and rolled over me.'

'The very worst fall a man can get. The horse is all right, I saw him yesterday.'

'Yes; I'm glad to hear that. It was the very first question I asked, as soon as I recollected anything about the business,' rejoined Mentmore. After a pause he added :—'By the way, Bradfield, how curiously things come about. This rather severe cropper will serve a good purpose. I have long wanted you to be more acquainted with Carrington; I think you would understand and appreciate one another; and I'm sure the ladies of the family would.'

Bradfield put on his usual peculiar smile, and then said—

'My father has his prejudices; but I have made some advances myself, lately. I've been to see Miss Carrington.'

'Miss Carrington?' and Lord Mentmore stared, and smiled too.

'I mean the lady known as Miss Philly Carrington.'

'Oh—oh—oh! I see. A charming person, but scarcely a young man's companion.'

'On the contrary; I enjoy her conversation much. Quaint, epigrammatic, and full of anecdotes of a former period. She interests me exceedingly.'

Mentmore hesitated a moment, as if he was doubtful how far he might proceed; but a short time had produced a more rapid intimacy than usual, perhaps from their earlier acquaintance, and he said in a lower voice,—

'I should have thought the other Miss Carrington more likely to have interested you than Aunt Philly.'

'Ah!' said the other, dryly enough, but without changing his habitual look of indifference or light-heartedness; 'there's no accounting for tastes. Besides, Miss Carrington is unapproachable by any but the *haute noblesse.*'

'Indeed you make a great mistake, my dear fellow; and, if that was a gentle hit at me, you were never more wrong in your life.'

'Is it so?'

'It is so, indeed. No one can know her without liking her. Her beauty alone is sufficiently attractive; her charming temper, and manners, so thoroughly ladylike and unaffected; and as to the *haute noblesse*, I believe that to be the very last thing she thinks of in a husband.'

Laurence Bradfield knew Lord Mentmore well enough to know that he was speaking the truth, and that had he not been intending to do so, he never would have broached the subject. He looked, however, steadily at him for some seconds, while the young earl examined the seals of his letters.

'Do you know that you are not to read too much at present?'

'Yes; I did hear so; but letters accumulate; I must run through them. Ah! here's my good aunt, Lady Elizabeth Derwentwater—three days without an answer;' and he rang a handbell, at which summons his valet appeared from an inner room:—'Bring my writing materials, Watkins, and put them down here.'

'And must you write to Lady Elizabeth to-day?'

'Indeed, I must; she'll be quite distressed. She is the only person who ever tries to control me, and to whom I am indebted for occasional contradiction.'

'Let me write, and say how unwell you have been.'

'My dear fellow, you'd have her ladyship here to-morrow.'

'I am sure my mother would be very happy.'

'Then your mother would be very different from me, and the rest of us too, I imagine. She's a clever woman—fond of management. Let her do all that at Silvermere and Derwent; there's plenty of room for her genius.'

'I have not the pleasure of Lady Elizabeth's acquaintance, but—'

'I hope you soon will have. This very letter, which you object to, is about my Easter invitations, over which my aunt presides. I am in hopes of persuading yourselves to be of my party. We must find something to do for a fortnight before the London season, so I hope I may count upon you and Mrs. and Miss Bradfield.'

'Thank you, you're very good; I have no doubt that my mother and sister will be very happy, and I shall endeavour to enjoy the recess.' And then he left his sick friend to his own devices.

The illness of Lord Mentmore had induced an interchange of civilities between Sommerton and Spring Vale. It was necessary that it should do so. The old people did not meet. Sir Michael called upon Lord Mentmore, and left a card on the hall-table: his passing civility was understood to be a necessity, and not returned. But the rest of them got on well enough; and Laurence had evidently taken Spring Vale Cottage by storm. He was very constant in his visits; and it is only just to say that Aunt Philly encouraged him to repeat them.

Mentmore recovered as rapidly as a nobleman attended by three doctors could possibly be expected to recover. He found Sommerton a pleasant residence enough, and, as he regained strength, accompanied the ladies in their drives, or Laurence and his sister in their rides. He did not return immediately to Spring Vale nor to Silvermere. In point of fact, he found a strong attraction in the society of Miss Bradfield to remain longer, and was willing to believe that politeness required a prolongation of his visit. Mentmore had never been taught to thwart himself, and he considered it almost a divine excellence to bear the occasional thwarting of others.

Laurence Bradfield went frequently to Spring Vale Cottage. He was a remarkably clever person, and old Aunt Philly enjoyed his conversation as much as he did hers. He occasionally saw Evelyn Carrington there, and his pleasure was not lessened by that circumstance. Occasionally when she rose to go, he would take his leave at the same time, and accompany her as far as the garden gate. There their roads diverged; she turned up towards the Manor Lodge, he down to the left along Water Lane—a short and cheerful walk through the fields to Sommerton.

'Aunt, that young Bradfield, who has just been returned for Plumpton, is not such a bad fellow after all,' said the Reverend Walter Carrington.

'Then, Walter, you'd better imitate him.'

'He's a dreadful Radical.'

'Is he? He often comes in here, and I never have found it out.'

'He would hardly bring his politics with him to Spring Vale.'

'I think he carries his opinions about with him for everyday wear: your idea is, that they are, like most people's religion, kept for holiday use.'

'He'll be a great man some day,' rejoined the parson.

'And a good one, nephew, if I know anything of character.'

'He ought to marry well, aunt; it would give him a good start in the county.'

'Perhaps he will, Walter; it's high time you set him the example.'

'Can't afford it, my dear madam.'

'Yes, you can, sir: I'll tell you how. Sell your hunters, and get rid of your curate; your wife will do the weekly duties of the latter.'

It was a little remarkable that Evelyn Carrington never mentioned his name.

'Stafford, what book is that you are so deep in?' said Evelyn, one morning.

'Hallam,' said Stafford, looking up affectionately from his book in the beautiful library of Spring Vale Manor; 'Hallam.'

'What's that about?'

'A great many things.'

'What? the way to preserve foxes or pheasants?'

'Foxes or pheasants! No; constitutions.'

'What? on training—that the papers are so full of since the last boat-race?'

'No, no, my dear Evelyn; not physical constitutions—political.'

'Oh! politics. How stupid I am. Then you mean to start, on papa's retirement, for the county; and you are preparing for it?'

'Not exactly that, perhaps; but it becomes one to be well informed.'

'I thought you were well informed, Stafford; everybody says so.'

'How kind. I thought so too, but I have found out that I am not.'

'What do you call a well-informed man?'

'I call young Bradfield a well-informed man. They speak very highly of him at the Parthenopeium, and deservedly so. It must be a nuisance to him to be so rich.'

'Why so?' said Evelyn, who could not comprehend that inconvenience.

'Because it must be so difficult to do anything with no motive for exertion.'

Mrs. Bradfield sat at breakfast; and Mr. Bradfield, after opening his letters, and cursing the tea, for the adulteration of which he declared that Alderman S—— ought to be hanged, opened a conversation.

'Who dines here to-day besides Lord Mentmore?'

'Nobody that I know of, unless you have asked some one.'

'I expect Lord Holocaust by the three o'clock train from town, and his son Lord Frederick Derrynane. They will be here about five; the carriage must be at the station. Next week I expect Sir Alexander and Lady Muscatel, the late Lord Mayor, Mr. and Mrs. Bertrand Smythe, Sir Peter Foozle, and the Duc de Belle Alliance. He's a very distinguished member of the ex-royal family. Everything must be got ready for him, and he will be treated like a crowned head while here. He stays two days to see my books.'

Mrs. Bradfield felt very uncomfortable; but, as most women do, trusted to the chapter of accidents, and said she would do her best.

'You know what Lord Holocaust is coming here for, I suppose?'

'I have heard you say, with a view to proposing his son for Ellen. Does she know anything of it herself?'

'Not unless you've told her, which you're just fool enough to do. What is it to her? What time does Lord Mentmore usually appear?' asked Abel Bradfield, with a frown.

The fact is, Ellen knew all about it.

'Usually at luncheon—not before. He still looks very weak.'

'It's very unlucky that Lord Holocaust should come now, just as Lord Mentmore is recovering,' said Bradfield.

'It cannot make much difference, I should think; they will be company for one another. I'm sure Lord Mentmore must find it stupid enough. Is Laurence coming down to the dinner?' replied his wife.

'Your son, madam, does not condescend to consult me; and as I have not asked him, he will probably be here.'

Mr. Bradfield walked out as Ellen Bradfield, looking as lovely as only an Englishwoman can look at nine o'clock in the morning, walked in and took her seat.

'Do you know that Lord Holocaust and his son are coming here to-day, Ellen?'

'I have heard something about it, mamma.'

'Have you been told the object of his visit, my love?'

'I think I know, mamma,' said Ellen, blushing, and looking a little pained.

'My dear, your father has set his heart on this.'

'I don't think it has much to do with *his* heart, dear mamma; and I feel little inclination to sell mine. However, we need not trouble about it yet.'

'That's just what I say. Nobody knows what may happen, dear. Don't you think, Ellen, it would be a good opportunity to invite the Carringtons to dinner, to make up our quarrel, while Lord Mentmore is here?'

'Leave the Carringtons to ask us, if they wish for our acquaintance. What is to be done with Lord Mentmore to-day? Laurence is in town.'

'He must go out in the carriage, unless he will ride. I can't think, Ellen dear, why he doesn't ride that quiet pony that he sent for last week.'

Ellen did not enlighten her mother as to the probable cause. We will.

Lord Mentmore was falling in love; and seeing no pleasanter method of passing the day than in the society of Miss Bradfield, he simply rode when he could ride with her, and was always too weak to ride by himself on the days when Laurence Bradfield was away. He was quite sure to prefer the carriage this afternoon, and Miss Bradfield was very conscious of the fact.

'Sir Michael, wait a moment before you go out. Don't you think it would be a good opportunity to make some advance to the Bradfields, while Lord Mentmore is with them? Shall we ask them to dinner next week?' said Lady Carrington.

'D— the Bradfields, my dear; but do just as you please,' said Sir Michael; keeping to himself the comforting assurance that he had quite prevented the possibility of Abel Bradfield's acceptance of her invitation.

While these scenes of every-day life were enacting, two persons were pre-eminently uncomfortable; and they certainly deserved to be so. One was Dan Morton, the other was Abel Bradfield. The first of these carried about with him his own incubus. He had struggled for it; and now that he had got it, in the shape of a parchment, as he was pleased to call it, he did not know what to do with it. It was his constant companion. No familiar could have been more faithful; nor could he have hugged his dearest friend with greater solicitude; for he carried it about all day in his velveteen shooting-coat, and placed it under his pillow at night, where it did not tend to soothe his slumbers. But I think I have said all that before. The only solace to his wounded spirit was in fresh depredations, which he still committed on the lands of his patron, Abel Bradfield, almost with impunity. He firmly believed in the intrinsic value of his stolen property; but he was impatient, and unable, to realize.

Abel Bradfield, since his visit to Hugh Darville, had been singularly irritable even for him. Perhaps for the first time in his life he had got some advice which he meant to follow, and was quite unable to do so. 'Burn it, burn it, if you burn the house down,' was the warning he listened to. But before he could burn it, it must be found. So day after day, as opportunity offered, the search went on, but the missing paper could no where be found. What if it should already have been destroyed! Possibly it might have been; but by whom? At first he searched the house from head to foot; his private room was then devoted to the more careful scrutiny of such documents as offered any hope; still he was unsuccessful. For some days he was urged to renewed exertions; until at length an useless restlessness took possession of him, and he wandered from room to room of his vast mansion, with a despairing scowl upon his hard features. And he was unable to ask for assistance in his search or sympathy in his loss, which made the case only worse.

But there is scarcely any constitution which has not some remedy for its exigencies. In the midst of his dissembled terrors he was to receive visitors. Had these been ordinary persons, with no interest attaching to them but that of his usual guests, they would only have increased his irritation. But they were to forward one of his great schemes. They were people well known in fashionable life, and whose countenance would at least give him a step towards his favourite projects of self-elevation. Lord Mentmore was with him, accidentally it is true; but what an accident! Lord Holocaust and his son had announced their intended visit, and with what a purpose! the ex-Lord Mayor and his wife, a city man truly, but distinguished above all city men, —shall I say by his pompous vulgarity and immense fortune? and the Duc de Belle

Alliance. H.R.H. were cabalistic letters almost capable of charming anything or anybody. 'Lord Mentmore! Lord Mentmore! an earl descended from the Tudors, with a rent-roll of seventy thousand a year,' said the manufacturer to himself, 'why might not he have done for his daughter?' and he forthwith began to despise the Holocaust alliance, as heartily as he had desired it. 'At least they might have put off their visit for another week or two. But could one ever have calculated on such an event?' No! nothing, not even his successes, went right with him.

CHAPTER II.

A LITTLE SOCIETY, QUITE A 1.

'Suche dir die wahrhaften Vorzüge der guten Gesellschaft, wo du zugelassen wirst, anzueignen.'—*Deuts. Maxn.*

THE Duc de Belle Alliance arrived in due course of time at Sommerton. If he is a man fond of attention, he must have been much gratified. His outward demeanour, however, rather falsified that notion. For two days he was bored to death. He was brought from the station in the finest carriage and with the finest horses (four of them to do two miles) that Mr. Abel Bradfield's well-stocked purse could furnish. The carriage indeed was a fine ex-sheriff's vehicle, hired for the occasion. He was literally bowed from the door of the railway carriage, through a host of officials and retainers, by Mr. Abel Bradfield himself, who remained uncovered throughout the ceremony in spite of the remonstrances of Monseigneur. He was made to ascend into this city conveniency, where the excellent Duc was compelled to sit in state; and Abel Bradfield, his host, followed by himself at an humble distance in his own private brougham. Arrived at the Hall the same terrible ceremonies awaited him from the assembled guests, who had sacrificed their own sense of decorum to the earnest solicitations of the master of the house. Nothing occurred to mar the beauty of these arrangements, but the absence of Lord Mentmore, who was too formidable to be taken into consultation on the subject; and the fall of the stout and somewhat infirm Mr. Timmins, the butler, in his attempt to back up the stone steps of the portico. The Duc nearly tripped over him, and very good humouredly held out his hand to raise the fallen worshipper. He was highly delighted when he arrived safely indoors, and was allowed to pay his respects to the ladies in his own way, who received him at the top of the aforesaid steps.

A foreign duke, of the ex-royal family of his own country, is a great personage for Mr. Abel Bradfield to have received as a guest at Sommerton. It was a relief to find that that eminent man was a much better-bred person than his host, and that he fell at once into an easy conversation, which put everybody at their ease, unless we except Sir Alexander Muscatel, and what he called his lady, *autrefois* his wife. These two could not be made comfortable even by the *bonhomie* and elegance of so well-bred a man as the Duc de Belle Alliance. Lord Holocaust and his son had seen royal dukes before, notwithstanding their expatriation, as they called, curiously enough, a lengthened residence in Ireland. Mr. Bertrand Smythe, *né* Smith, and his wife, were not people to be abashed by anything, and believed that an Englishman was equal to the whole nobility of the Continent put together. Mrs. Bradfield's gentle and unaffected simplicity of manner was her best guarantee for never committing herself, and Ellen Bradfield never shone more conspicuously than when her talents for society were called into play.

The Duc, himself one of the most, perhaps the most, accomplished man of the age, had a happy tact of saying a few words on subjects likely to meet the capacity and tastes of everybody. To the ladies, obviously the house, its beauties and curiosities; to his host, who was busied about many things, his books, his farm, his ironworks (of which he was honestly ashamed by the way), afforded topics of conversation.

'Lord Holocaust: I think we have met before, at Lady ——'s.'

It was a flattering reminiscence on the part of the Duc. Lord Frederick Derrynane was presented personally; he bowed smilingly, stroked his moustaches which were handsome, and hoped Monseigneur had enjoyed his journey.

'Yes! indeed,' said His Royal Highness, with but little accent, 'the country is very fine, and the weather not cold, that is, for the season.'

'Sir Alexander Muscatel and Lady Muscatel,' said Mrs. Bradfield.

All stood still, as the Duc was not yet seated; and as he preferred warming himself with his back to the fire on the hearth-rug, it was not quite clear whether they were to spend the next two hours in an upright position.

The Duc immediately inquired the fashionable news at the West-end, knowing that he could not more highly flatter an ex-lord mayor than by ignoring the city altogether. After a few more disjointed sentences, everyone began to wish that Lord Mentmore would arrive, quite satisfied that they should then see the proper way to meet a Duc of the blood royal; and he did arrive just in the nick of time.

'Ah! mon cher Mentmore,' said the Duc at once, rushing forward to embrace his friend. 'You here? That is a pleasure.'

'Yes, monseigneur. I am indebted to Mr. and Mrs. Bradfield for a long visit, and for great kindness after a bad fall. I have been laid up here;' and then commenced the most natural conversation in the world, about hunting, shooting, dukes, marquises, London, Paris, and the hundred-and-one things which intimates do talk about. Sir Alexander and Lady Muscatel were astonished, and Mr. and Mrs. Bertrand Smith flattered to find that a royal duke, after all, talked and looked very like other people. Indeed His Royal Highness began to lose caste, or something akin to it. The present remaining semblance of royalty was rather an uncomfortable one—that all stood round him on the hearth-rug, as if he had been the Lincolnshire fat boy, the learned pig, or Miss Biffin.

Having arrived at the fact that he might be talked to without any great danger of a *lettre de cachet* and the Bastille, Sir Alexander Muscatel cleared his throat for action; and a lull having come after a good joke of Lord Mentmore's, at which the Duc laughed heartily, it appeared a good opportunity for saying something. Having made up his mind that he was expected to say something about his own doings with great people, and having been on the deputation of city aldermen, who had represented that portion of London before his Majesty the Emperor of ——, with a pomposity of voice and manner, and with an effect which was perfectly electrical, he inquired of His Royal Highness 'Whether he was acquainted with his Majesty the Emperor of ——, as he had passed several days at the ——, and he had found him a most charming and affable person?'

The faces of all the people in the room, excepting that of the royal personage addressed, assumed a very extraordinary change from gay to grave. The Duc, however, stroked the large imperial he wore, and answered with great calmness, and a sly look at Mentmore, which produced a laugh on that nobleman's countenance—

'That he had the honour of his acquaintance, but that circumstances prevented them from meeting so often, or fraternizing so intimately, as they might have done.'

Taking compassion upon the terrified looks of Abel Bradfield, who cursed all the aldermen in the world at the same moment of time, the Duc referred to his library, and mentioned some rare edition of the 'Epistles of Abelard,' which was understood to be in Mr. Abel Bradfield's possession.

Having relieved Sir Alexander Muscatel of his difficulty, the Duc at length threw himself into a chair which was at hand, and took up 'The Times.' Lord Mentmore took possession of a pamphlet; and the ladies followed one another out of the room. Retired grocers are very respectable people, but they ought to arm themselves with the weapons of society, the Peerage, Foreign, Colonial, and British, before they enter upon the arena of conversation with foreign dukes.

The two days of this distinguished meeting passed over pleasantly and rapidly. There were farms and improvements to be inspected; machinery and iron-works, early cucumbers, valuable Elzevirs, illuminated missals, rare copies of rarer pictures, as subjects of conversation, an afternoon's drive, which the Duc divested of some of its formality by requesting permission to accompany the ladies, and which deprived Lord Frederick Derrynane of his seat in the carriage, Lord Mentmore occupying the vacant space next to the Duc. There were some horses to be looked at; and had there been some to be ridden, Monseigneur would willingly have given up the Aldines and Elzevirs, for which he was ostensibly Abel Bradfield's guest. As it was, he retired to the stable with Mentmore, and smoked his cigar after breakfast without regretting the absence of his host. Even indoors he liked his room better than his company. Dinner, under such circumstances, is a heaven-born institution indeed. At all times such a thing is acceptable. Whether it consists of a potato, a pipe, and a go of whisky, or the most elaborate performance of Soyer, Ude, or Francatelli; whether it be taken under a hedge in a gipsy tent, in a puddle at a pic-nic (this we take to be the worst possible form), or in a Belgravian dining-room, the result is the same. It supplies a want. Among the wealthy it is far more valuable, strange anomaly! than with the poor. The tinker satisfies nothing but his hunger, as he sits beneath the sweet-smelling curtains of the hawthorn tree sheltered from a summer's sun. The dinner of a gentleman is intended to satisfy half-a-dozen wants, and oh! rarity for this world! answers its purpose. His hunger, his vanity, his prejudices, above all things his *ennui*, are satisfied by his dinner.

Having bored your friends, and having been bored by them, from 9 A.M. to 7.30 P.M., it is a proud position to sit opposite to one's wife, supported on either sidé by a royal duke and a puissant earl. As Abel Bradfield sat down to this delicacy, he was a proud man. To some it might have occurred that his position was the greater, that he had arrived at it in spite of external circumstances. It ought to have been a subject of congratulation, that his father being a nobody, and his grandfather having no existence at all, he was the host of princes and the possessor of boundless resources. He could not shut his eyes to the advantages of his fine rooms, handsome pictures, burning lights, and sumptuous fare, but he would have been prouder of it all, had he acquired it by no industry, no talents, no perseverance, in himself or his father. He would like the honour and its source to have been further apart. He was not a man to believe that, in the absence of abstract qualities, the heat is more intense, and therefore more valuable, before its radiation. He would have given a certain portion, even of the substance, for some of the shadow; and enjoyed a name which had been made for him by the virtues of a mediæval ancestor, far more than one attainable by his own. I do not like those men. I love hereditary titles to respect to be accompanied by a practical claim upon mankind; and I know that they frequently are; but I love, even beyond it, an innate sense of virtue and honour, which will strive to make for itself a name and rights truly divine, by exertions employed for the good of our fellow-creatures.

Abel Bradfield had none of the latter feelings, he was proud only that his wife sat between the Duc de Belle Alliance and Lord Mentmore, and rather ashamed of the reason why.

'Ah! mi Lord Mentmore; you are well, here. The house is good, the cuisine is good, and the daughter of our friend is *superbe.*' Royal dukes are human.

'You think so, monseigneur; the young lady will be flattered,' rejoined Mentmore.

'Yes: you think so—truly she is charming. You English are very proud of your aristocracy. Here is our man of iron presents you with a model for countesses.'

'But in our country we make countesses of them.'

'A mesalliance,' said the democratic royalist.

'There need be none. In England there are other patents of nobility besides birth.'

'Wealth and talents,' replied the Duc; 'but you think nothing of them.'

'Plaît-il, monseigneur? pardon me. For the first we have the greatest reverence; the second requires but one generation to be forgotton in the natural claims of a title; a combination of the two overrides the other; and the possession of all these is—' Lord Mentmore hesitated for a word.

'Irresistible,' interposed the foreigner. 'Yours is an enviable position, mi Lord Mentmore.'

'Your highness thinks so?'

'Certainly; you can convert anything into the Countess of Mentmore.'

'You know Lord Frederick Derrynane?'

'No! but I see him here; why do you ask?'

'He is to convert our host's daughter, Miss Bradfield, into an earl's daughter-in-law, so that I, at least, have no chance of the result your highness proposes.'

'Then we must not take Derrynane's seat in the carriage again to-day. We shall ride;' and accordingly they did so, while Lord Derrynane pushed his advances by those skilful means which are said never to fail, provided — there be no stronger army in the field, to relieve the place. There! that's sufficient, we need go no further down the list of 'ifs.'

'I hope your royal highness enjoyed your ride this afternoon. Lord Mentmore is an excellent pilot, I believe.'

'Very much indeed, thank you; we went through a fine country for hunting; the fields are very large between here and Spring Vale. My friend Sir Michael Carrington has also a fine place there,' said the duke, from the other end of the table.

'You have been there, monseigneur?'

'Yes, to-day. They are a charming family.' Abel Bradfield could scarcely conceal his vexation, but he choked his choler with a glass of wine, which did not rise high against a royal duke. 'We saw Miss Carrington, who is lovely; and Mr. Stafford Carrington was not at home. I dare say the young ladies are intimate?' added he, turning to Mrs. Bradfield.

'Not very,' replied that lady. 'Have you known Sir Michael long?'

'My acquaintance is more with Lady Carrington, who used to be much abroad at one time. She was frequently in Paris.'

'Charming place, Paris,' began Sir Alexander Muscatel, who was about to give the company some of his experiences of Parisian life, when he was cut short by one of the chance guests, who said 'hot,' and another, who remarked 'that depends on the time of year, cold enough in winter.'

'You should go to Egypt,' said Bertrand Smythe, though he did not say why, and as nobody seemed anxious to attach this general remark to himself, it fell to the ground.

Miss Bradfield inquired of Lord Frederick whether he knew the Carringtons. 'Yes! he did a little. Faith! Carrington gave himself airs. Not his style of man at all.' The duke also told the company, that he had ridden from Spring Vale, round by Saxonby, where he had inspected the national schools, the church, and the union workhouse: a lively occupation, to which royal dukes, especially foreigners, are handed over by their friends.

'Any news in Saxonby, Lord Mentmore?' said Mr. Bradfield, anxious to say something. Royal dukes are not supposed to understand county politics, but he answered with great readiness, 'We heard that Sir Michael Carrington was going to—to—give up—what you call retire from Parliament; and that his son would take his place.' Lord Mentmore continued to eat without confirming or contradicting this intelligence; but no apple of discord could have produced greater effect than this did upon Abel Bradfield. However, there was nothing to be done but to grin and bear it, which he did, like a bear at a stake.

The dinner was half over when the servant threw open the door, and Laurence Bradfield walked up to his mother, and saluted her. He was presented to the Duc, who greeted him cordially. He then made a general salutation to the company, with an apology for not having arrived earlier. 'Business of the House;' and a side-table was prepared, from which the young man talked, and ate, and drank alternately.

'Business of the House!' Here was a pretty way to treat a prince of the ex-royal family of ——, thought Mr. Bradfield, sen., 'business of the House. What house! certainly it was not the business of the house of Bradfield to do so.' And as if this little pill was not bitter enough, it caused him once more to reflect upon the intelligence with which the Duc had just enlightened the table. Laurence Bradfield continued to eat and drink, as if there were no such thing as a royal duke or a vacant seat in Parliament.

Before they retired for the night Mentmore announced his intended departure, 'the day after the next.' The rest of the guests were to terminate their visits about the same time, the great lion of the meeting being due at some other showman's on the morrow. Thus the coast was to be left clear for the premeditated movement of Lord Frederick Derrynane. Poor fellow! he was not bad in himself—not more vicious than two-thirds of the fellows who had been at Eton with him; but circumstances had made him half a fool, and other circumstances had tended to keep him half a knave.

The first half of his nature blinded him to the fact that such a girl as Ellen Bradfield was not likely to unite herself to the whole which two such halves presented; and when he did find it out, the most flattering unction he could lay to what he called his heart was that Mentmore had forestalled him. What made the matter worse was that when rejection came, which of course it did in course of time, and in a manner as delicate as it was decided, he could not help exhibiting his want of generosity.

'Is there no hope that—that time perhaps—haw—ha-a—'

'None whatever, Lord Frederick; in such a matter it is better for me to be candid, and to state that I do not feel that time could change the purport of my answer.'

'Ah! Miss Bradfield; I am unfortunate,' replied he rather bitterly, instead of appreciating the honesty which was intended to save him useless pain, 'had I but known beforehand of the—the—haw—pre-occupation—ha-a.'

'My lord, I really do not understand your meaning.'

'Ha—ha—of course—haw—Lord Mentmore—his appearance here may have—ha—ha—prejudiced.'

Ellen Bradfield drew herself up, as well she might, and looking Lord Frederick Derrynane straight in the face, she said,

'I can only understand your meaning now, my lord, to be one of intentional insult. Permit me to assure you that if Lord Mentmore had never been born, it would have made not the slightest difference in any sentiments I may have expressed towards you. I beg to wish your lordship a very good morning;' and Miss Bradfield walked rather decidely up to her own apartments, leaving Lord Frederick Derrynane with the gratifying assurance that he might order his portmanteau to be packed at once.

In the meantime Mentmore himself thought a great deal about his visit to Sommerton; and perhaps the strongest symptom he discovered of admiration for his late host's daughter was to be found in an increased dislike to Lord Frederick. It was a sort of negative acquiescence in the promptings of his inclination rather than a good wholesome principle of love for a beautiful and generous girl. Mentmore, I have said, was very much spoilt about women, and had been made suspicious; so that with many charming traits of character, he had his faults, and a shyness of susceptibility was one of them. He was, however, as usual, immersed in business. Long absence from home brought an accumulation of tenants, bailiffs, stewards, head-keepers, stud-grooms, and above all his master of the horse, who had run over from Newmarket to have a chat about the horses, and to report upon the favourite for the Two Thousand.

'How is Stonehenge?'—he was a magnificent colt by the Druid out of Idolatry.

'Looking wonderful—he had a three-mile gallop this morning, and I saw him again this evening, before I came away,' said Wilfred Jones, a man who had spent all his money and all his time on the turf, and having nothing to do of his own, was now looking after Lord Mentmore's stud at Newmarket. It was no sinecure, and Wilfred Jones found it none. It ought to be acknowledged that he tried to do his duty.

'Ground in good order?' asked his lordship.

'Capital; and he does strong work now; he wants nothing but the last polish.'

'Have you anything on your own account, Wilfred?'

'Oh! a trifle—of course I've backed him.'

'You needn't do so any more; I've put you on. You can have a tenner with me;' and Mentmore pulled out his book.

'There's not much chance of my doing any more. I called at Tattersall's as I came by, and some one has been before us.'

'The devil there has!' said Mentmore, who was hasty at times, of course.

'I can't make it out, Mentmore; I wish I could, but there's something wrong; Jackson sells his information, or else he is circumvented by some scoundrel or other. The horse was at fourteen to one. After the private trial, the moment I got into the ring, I was offered nine, then seven, then five.'

'What did you do?'

'I took the nine in ponies, and offered to lay the five—no takers. I found out that Jackson has lately had a visitor, a rough-looking customer; one of his former pals; and anything like that must be very bad form indeed. It must be stopped, or no good can be done with the stable. I'm afraid you stand a good lump this time?'

'More than I can afford,' said his lordship, a thing he seldom admitted. 'However, if it comes off right—'

'Dinner is served, my lord,' said a servant throwing open the door; so Jones and Lord Mentmore finished their conversation over their wine.

CHAPTER III.

THE FIRST APPROACHES.

'Under floods that are deepest,
Which Neptune obey,
Over rocks that are steepest
Love will find out the way.'—*Old Song.*

It was a very bright, hard-blowing day in March. The trees were bending to something approaching a hurricane, and the clouds flitted past in rapid succession, chasing one another through the sky. Laurence Bradfield was down in the country for a few days, having had rather a hard time of it at St. Stephen's. Weather was of little consequence to him; and having invited his sister to a walk with him, which she had declined, he took his way alone to the cottage at Spring Vale, pretty sure of finding its owner at home on such a day. For once he was mistaken. The old lady was out.

'And where is Miss Carrington gone, Nurse? I am anxious to see her to-day.'

'I imagine she may be up at the Hall, sir,' replied her favoured domestic.

'Then I'll call again by-and-by.' Laurence Bradfield did not think it necessary to say that he had not yet the *entrée* to those holy precincts.

'Very good, sir,' said Nurse, and shut the door with difficulty in the face of the March wind, which carried a whirlwind of dust into the square hall.

Laurence Bradfield walked into the village, and turning up the hill approached the rectory; as he came opposite to it the gate opened and Evelyn Carrington came out. They greeted each other kindly, and Bradfield looked down upon the light-hearted girl with a curious interest.

At that moment she looked exceedingly pretty. Indeed, it is not certain that many men would not have preferred her to Miss Bradfield. The colour in her cheeks, the smiling dimples, the rounded chin and feminine mouth with its dainty pearls within, the glossy hair now dishevelled in front by the boisterous wind, and the laughing, love-beaming brown eyes with their long dark lashes, were all external signs of the happy disposition and affectionate heart which endeared Evelyn Carrington to everybody around her. These are not, however, generally the signs of the highest class of English beauty. They usually accompany a lower conformation of character, a lower type of mind. Whence comes it, then, that Evelyn escaped this defect? From the natural simplicity by which every action was accompanied, and by a beauty and delicacy of figure not inferior to that of Ellen Bradfield herself. If the latter was fitter to share the council-chamber and the throne of a king, the former looked more like the mother of his children, the participator in his domestic happiness. If dignity and easy greatness sat well upon Ellen Bradfield, a cheerful brightness and sunshine distinguished Evelyn Carrington wherever she appeared.

'Miss Carrington,' said he, crossing a remarkably muddy road which was, however, drying by the wind; 'it's long since we met. In fact, not since the day of the eventful run when Lord Mentmore hurt himself.'

'No; have you heard of or from him lately?'

'Not a word;' and here Laurence looked at her. If he expected a tell-tale blush or any other change, he was doomed to be disappointed. 'Mentmore has too many irons in the fire for much letter-writing.'

'Not more than yourself, I should think. Surely, Mr. Bradfield, you are the busiest man of the two.'

'I think not. The largest hunting establishment in England, a string of horses at Newmarket, forty thousand acres of deer-forest in Scotland, with what shooting and fishing I know not besides; a large house in town, and three in the provinces, with a villa at Como, and thousands of tenants and dependants amongst whom he is to distribute some hundred thousand a year, is a busier man than the

Member for Plumpton.' They continued to walk side by side till they came to the gate of Miss Philly's cottage, where they stopped walking, but continued to talk.

'Perhaps he may be. He ought to be, certainly. I wonder if he's happier for it all?'

'A man can only partially command happiness, Miss Carrington, whoever or whatever he may be.'

'I cannot help liking Lord Mentmore so much, that I never think he makes enough of himself. His resources are so very great.'

'Everybody likes him, and I doubt not he might be a greater and a wiser man; but who could not? At the same time, it must be allowed that no man spends money so gracefully and so fearlessly, and surely that was one of the purposes for which he came into the world.'

'But too much on himself,' said Miss Carrington.

'You desire to distinguish between self-love and selfishness; but Lord Mentmore cannot help appearing selfish, when he may be acting for the simple benefit of others.'

'But he would be as well with a twentieth part of the horses, and a third of the houses; he can neither ride them all nor live in them.'

'That proves his disinterestedness. He cannot use all he has, a third of the numbers he has, but he keeps them for the good of trade and the benefit of his friends.'

'Ostentation?' said Miss Carrington.

'You like to hear me defend him. He wants a more powerful advocate, at least an honester one.'

'Why should you say that, Mr. Bradfield?'

'Because—' and here he paused and looked down, but as if determined to look the affair straight in the face, he raised his eyes again and met hers; 'because I would prefer to plead for myself to you.'

If the words could have been misunderstood, the tone in which they were spoken could not. Evelyn turned her head, and blushed scarlet. It was impossible for her to answer immedi ately, so utterly unexpected had been the turn which the conversation had taken. Bradfield continued with rapid utterance:

'Oh! Evelyn, forgive me if I have offended you; the opportunities I have had of seeing you lately left me no alternative but to tell you. Perhaps I am premature, it may require time to efface certain prejudices; but give me hope, and then see the name which I am capable of making, with such as you to share it.' The secret was out, and in plain enough language now; and Evelyn Carrington hung her head in the silence, not of displeasure, but almost of despair.

And how was it possible to tell him without offence?—and how could she offend one of whom she knew nothing but good, and who loved her, as she had guessed indeed long before?

'Mr. Bradfield, you don't know—there are circumstances which make it so difficult for me to answer properly;' and here she hesitated and fairly broke down. The heavy tears hung on the lids that had never known sorrow before, as she began to feel all the happiness she was doomed to lose.

He interrupted her, and took her hand, which she did not withdraw, and then turning away from her so as not to be witness to her distress, he said, 'Yes; I know there are circumstances—but why should there be? There are prejudices of birth to be overcome; but may not honesty, and wealth, and learning in this country create a title to respect? There are sorenesses which have rankled long in the hearts of our fathers, but must they be perpetuated in us? Ask your aunt's advice—'

'There is no one like my mother; you do not know her; but my own sense tells me that I ought not to listen longer.'

'But you—you are not ashamed of an honest man's love?'

'I ashamed? oh no! but you scarcely know—'

And at that moment old Aunt Philly appeared at a cottage-door about thirty paces from the gate on which the lovers were leaning. Evelyn Carrington turned to go, with one look of affection, which held out but small expectation of success, and Laurence Bradfield crossed the road to Aunt Philly.

The ice was broken, and it looked very much as if they were likely to drift beneath it.

'You have been faithless lately, Mr. Bradfield.'

'To you I have, Miss Carrington,' said Laurence, who had recovered his equanimity by an effort. In fact, his was a cheerful disposition, which never saw the impossibility of anything; the having started on the race seemed to him an earnest of winning. 'I have been away, in town.'

'Doing your duty.'

'You hardly think so.'

'I beg your pardon. I should like to see you with other views of what your duty is, sir; but I don't think you do it the less heartily because you are wrong. Saul made a vigorous convert, and so would you.'

Laurence smiled in the faint, half-mocking manner so peculiarly his. He never laughed; but a light came into his eyes, which he must have known was becoming to him.

'That's a left-handed compliment. You must regard me as very bad, Miss Carrington.'

'I regard you as very good among the very bad: there, sir, will that satisfy you? Now tell me the news, for my nephew is too busy to come and see an old woman.'

'Ah! immersed in politics. I hear he is to succeed Sir Michael in the county. A malignant still, you know; but less vicious.'

'Is there to be an opposition?'

'Certainly not on my part, and I know of none. I have neither heart nor part in the matter.'

'Truly then, Mr. Laurence, I ought to have less confidence in your goodness than I had. I thought you were bound to fight always.'

'I declined the combat once before, and am about to do so again. Need I be dissatisfied with Plumpton?'

'No, sir; but this county is a fine opening for an ambitious man.'

'Perhaps I'm not an ambitious man, Miss Carrington.'

'But I think you are an ambitious man, Mr. Bradfield.' And the old lady shook the stick which rested by her side at the speaker.

'For the sake of argument, granted; but must it be political? Might I not have another ambition—a more honest one than that of rivalry? If both sides could give a little and take a little, what good they might do. If Mr. Carrington descends a step from the pedestal of Sir Michael, Laurence Bradfield may come down from that of his father. There is a large class of moderate politicians rising, who shun the extremes of both parties, and who must eventually be the men of the day.'

'You think so, sir; and why?'

'Because they will be the advocates of discussion rather than opposition, and from among them only practical measures will come.'

The old lady shook her head. 'Don't believe it, sir. No country prospers without strong and marked partizanship—a powerful and unscrupulous minority keeps the Government on its best behaviour.' Perhaps the old lady was right, after all. 'Now, sir, does your ambition go no further than that?'

Laurence Bradfield had made great friends with Aunt Philly during the winter. He felt from the day of their walk in the fields that sort of respect which belongs, between persons of like dispositions, to sympathy. There was a great deal of affection mixed with it; and that she was Evelyn Carrington's aunt did not depreciate the old lady's value in his eyes. Rising, therefore, at this last question, and feeling that now or never he might interest her in his fortunes, he walked deliberately across the room, and placed himself opposite the fine roomy arm-chair which the little hunchbacked lady occupied.

'Yes, Miss Carrington, I have an ambition; and now forgive me if I offend you. I have not been able to see Miss Evelyn Carrington without feeling for her, long since, more than for any other lady of my acquaintance. I have been taught by the world that we tradesmen suffer under a peculiar disadvantage. I believe the teaching to be false, for I have never felt it; and in matters of sentiment the heart is the best instructor.' Miss Carrington was perfectly silent now, and rested her long chin upon the top of her ivory-crossed cane. 'You think differently, my dear madam; naturally you do. You were born to do so, and you have been educated to do so.' Still the old lady was silent. 'And that is why I ask your pardon. It is for offending your prejudices, Miss Carrington, not your convictions.' Her prejudices were giving way, but she had not yet arrived at any convictions. 'To be plain, I love your grand-niece, Miss Carrington. I would willingly be born again of a high and noble family, if I could, for her sake—but I can't. But I can do something more, perhaps better; I can make a name and a position apart from the wealth of a son of an unknown manufacturer, which a whole people shall be taught to reverence. Until I have advanced some steps upon my road, I shall not ask for my reward; when I do, I shall ask you to befriend me.'

There was much of enthusiasm—of fanaticism, if you will—in what Laurence Bradfield had said; but there was good, honest, sterling truthfulness at the bottom of it. As he stood erect before her, the light shone again in his blue eyes, and his broad chest swelled; and the little old lady put out her hand to him, and looked up with a kindness of which she was capable, but not lavish, and said,

'Laurence Bradfield, at present you can only have my good wishes; when the time arrives, you shall have my good word. Sit down; let us talk awhile.'

And so Laurence Bradfield sat down by Miss Carrington, and talked not altogether on indifferent subjects: that is to say, he spoke of his aspirations, his intentions, his hopes for his fellow-creatures; of the good he desired to do, and of the difficulty of setting about it in the right way; and he taught the old lady a lesson which all the Carringtons and most of their neighbours had to learn—the true difficulty with which the rich man has to contend on his road to heaven. It looks so very easy to do good when one has the means, and it is really so very hard; so that is the exercise of patience, and judgment, and tact, and consideration. Anybody can squander money, and very few can spend it.

And the old lady herself was not silent. She told him of the difficulties of his suit, and taught him what he did not understand—that the grievances were legion; that they were older than election opposition, and began when his grandfather had no opinions at all; that they were not only those of class, and of money (which is always a thorn with the losing side), but that there were definite, though unsubstantiated, charges against the early colonists of the Sommerton property, which, though they only affected the present generation collaterally, were positive offences in the eyes of those who suffered by them.

And as Miss Carrington related by scraps the same unvarnished tale which she has told once before in this book, Mr. Laurence Bradfield's eyes grew larger and larger; as his astonishment increased, his hopes grew less.

'And do you really mean to say, Miss Carrington, that my grandfather rested under such a suspicion of—what shall I call it?—meanness or treachery?'

'He did what was right in his own eyes: he bought up a poor man's interest in an estate, which he saw would repay the purchaser, as it has, hundreds per cent. Everybody in the same position would perhaps have done so. It wanted a large mind to resist. As to the payment of the loan by my brother, it rests on grounds that the world has long declared to be untenable, but which are clung to with increasing tenacity by a family which yearly feels the want of it more acutely. Now you see the difficulties you have to overcome. I know them well, and Evelyn knows them; it is but fair that you should know them too.'

CHAPTER IV.

A MYSTERIOUS AND UNSUCCESSFUL SEARCH.

'And so may I, blind fortune leading me,
Miss that which one unworthier may attain.'
Merch. of Venice.

MR. ABEL BRADFIELD sat late after breakfast. The ladies were gone, his son was in town, and he recreated himself with a second cup of tea, which Mr. Timmins had poured out for him, and 'The Times' newspaper, which, unlike Mr. Bright, he still continued to take, in spite of the cheaper dishes of literature and politics which have been served up of late years with the morning meal. He felt a considerable degree of interest in politics at all times; at least, he professed to do so. It is the correct thing, and a prudent thing, when men have arrived at colossal fortunes, which may be diminished or increased by the fluctuation of markets and the manœuvres of speculators.

At present he was more interested than usual, for he read a brilliant leader on a debate in which his son had taken a conspicuous part, and of whose praises, as a young member, the article in question was lavish. He had an idea that he had not done his son justice, now that he saw he was likely to be a great man without his assistance. He thought that he should be more considerate towards his failings, the chief of which seemed to be a determination to go his own way, and to break the bonds which ought to have enchained him to his father and the opinions of his party. His present effort on popular education was at least creditable to his brains and his eloquence, if it did not fully satisfy the demands of ultra-Radicalism, and the conclusion he came to was, that Laurence was henceforth to assume a position at home, which the world was bent upon giving him abroad.

Another reason for this tardy act of justice

was the ingratitude of his daughter. Ellen, the one thing he had cared about, and that more for the gratification of his vanity and schemes than for real love, had thwarted him; Ellen Bradfield would not be married to one coronet, and appeared entirely indifferent to the possibility of another. Ungrateful girl! She had done nothing to conciliate Lord Mentmore, and she had positively refused Lord Frederick Derrynane. To tell the truth, she seemed careless as to the claims of the whole British peerage; and, with all her beauty and hauteur, with her calm self-possession, so becoming the head of a ducal or baronial table, she looked very like throwing herself away upon whatever proved to be the object of her affections. Marriage was not a subject on which she often indulged in conversation, but when she did, her notions were peculiar, to say the least of it.

'The most despicable thing upon earth is a man or woman who marries for any reason but one—pure unbiassed affection.'

That was the only shot she fired during an animated contest on the subject, and Mr. Bradfield had not forgotten it.

At this moment his mind was occupied upon the desirability of patronizing his son and snubbing his daughter, and his teeth upon a piece of toast, when the door opened, and the servant announced Mr. Darville. He was closely followed by that gentleman.

'Good morning, Darville, glad to see you.' This extent of civility was caused by the instantaneous recollection that he required his services. 'Take a seat.'

The servant put one opposite the squire, and Darville took it.

'You've come about that business? Have you done anything?'

'I have.' But for once in his life the lawyer did not dive into his tail-coat pocket and produce a roll of papers, tied up with a piece of red tape. 'But not much.'

'Well! never mind; I'm sure you've done your best this time. What is it?'

'First let me tell you about the county. There can be no opposition.'

'D— the county, and the opposition too, sir. There can be none unless I offer it, and my son refuses to stand by me.' He looked in Darville's face, and he saw that his temper had got the better of his judgment, as it usually had done. 'I beg your pardon, however, but I am anxious about the other matter—those papers.'

'Not more anxious than I am, sir. They are not forthcoming, unless you have them. But I have gained some intelligence, since my interview with Scarsdale.'

'Scarsdale again?' and Bradfield half rose from his chair. 'What has he to do with it?'

'Something, at all events. He received old Morton's confession, if it may so be called; and, though he could make nothing of it, there was something in it, I can assure you.'

Abel Bradfield repeated the word 'Scarsdale' to himself several times. It certainly was an awkward business to have anything like a secret in the hands of Scarsdale, for Abel Bradfield judged most men by himself.

'But I told you this before, surely?'

He certainly never had; for Abel Bradfield was not the man to forget it.

'Never,' said he; 'and now what have you done, Darville?'

'I have ascertained that there is in your house a room, and that, if those documents are in existence, they are in that room.'

'And in which room do you suppose they are?'

Abel Bradfield had forgotten son, daughter, and everything else, in his anxiety to know.

'That, Mr. Bradfield, is for you to say. You must ascertain in which room old Morton Giles was likely to have been employed. It is the only clue we have.'

'Have you consulted his son?' demanded Abel Bradfield.

'He has disappeared. I have tracked him to Newmarket, but he was again away, and nothing further can be heard of him. I must ask you one or two questions, if we are to be certain that we are on no wild-goose chase. How are you assured of the existence of this document at all? All conjecture appears to me to be in favour of its destruction.'

'No, Darville, no. It was put away. The secret was in the hands of two or three, whose own safety was at stake, it is true; but still they knew the facts of the case. The destruction of the instrument itself would have finally compromised the whole. My father's dying breath declared its existence, and nothing but the suddenness of the last moments prevented its disclosure. Besides, he had a motive.'

'And that was?— if I may venture to ask.'

'A compromise, or future restitution. My father was actuated by nothing but a determination of making a fortune. Money would have induced him to do anything, and when you consider its power, who can be surprised at it? It is everything to all men. By keeping back the release, he held in his hands a means of compromise at all times. The worst come to the worst, he could have destroyed it at a moment's notice. If restitution would have paid him better, he had it in his power so long as he held that paper, and no longer. But I had it from his own lips: so far he got when a final paroxysm deprived him of speech, and I learnt no more. I learnt enough to know that I was in anybody's power, and with none of those safeguards of which my father held the key.' The very thought produced a terrible revulsion in Abel Bradfield, who, looking round at the luxury by which he was surrounded, saw no less plainly the uncertainty of his position. The contrast was the more striking between such boundless resources and his present helplessness.

'Then you require nothing but reassurance of possession,' said Darville, whose own participation, extending only to guilty knowledge, required nothing but the non-existence of the papers in question for his safety.

'On the contrary;' and Abel Bradfield's hard features showed, by the trembling lip and loss of colour, the malice that wrought within; 'on the contrary; if I could only be certain that they were gone—that they never could reappear for the benefit of the former possessor, even after my death—I could bear anything.' And then, forgetful of his former pride, which had concealed from his wife and daughter how bitterly he had suffered, he went on with a history of his wrongs. 'From the time I have lived in the county to the present day, he has made me feel his heel. He has insulted me before my brother magistrates, by contemptuous opposition or callous indifference. His wife and daughter have been taught to ignore the claims of the ladies of my family in public and private. As a neighbour, I owe him nothing but hostility. His cursed family, and their pre-eminence, have turned all hands against me. When I might have succeeded, he has thwarted me; when I would have done good, he has been beforehand with me. The very sight of him has made the waters bitter that might have been sweet. I have been more democratic than my nature, because he has been the embodiment of aristocratic pretensions. In his own house he has treated me with an insolence that was the more galling, because it could not be resented. Amid it all I have had but one pleasure, the recollection of the revenge I was taking, and I could die almost happy if I were well assured that he could know it hereafter. I have had but one pleasure—the contemplation of the straits to which he has been reduced by my father's treachery. Think of that, sir; think of that;' and the man laid his hand upon his heart, to still its beatings. 'What must I feel, when I tell you that I can set ignominy for the being who begot me, and for those who come after me in the scale, with my hatred towards Michael Carrington?' As Abel Bradfield concluded these words he sank into the chair he had quitted at the commencement of this discussion, and wiped, with trembling hands, the huge drops of perspiration which had settled on his brow.

Hugh Darville was thunderstruck—he was frightened; and pouring out a glass of water, from the caraffe which stood on the table, presented it to his friend. For some time neither spoke. The lawyer was unable to offer any counsel which could stem the tide of the other's indignation. Abel Bradfield had nothing more to say. At length he resumed, in a cold and trembling tone:—

'That paper I must have, Darville. Can you find it?'

'Everything shall be done that I can do to discover it; and if I could lay hands on Morton, I don't despair.'

'Spare no efforts; money shall be forthcoming. I have often had to modify the demands of that scoundrel, but this time he may name his price.'

'I don't know that he can assist us; I only hope so. He was with his father not long before his death, and there is a probability of his knowing something; at all events, he can tell us whether and where his father worked for Mr. Bradfield.'

At that moment a ray of light seemed to illumine Abel Bradfield's worn features. He was about to speak, but, with a strong effort, he repressed his first effort, and merely thanked him for his assistance. In a few minutes the lawyer took his leave.

He was scarcely gone—the echo of his footsteps had scarcely died away from the marble flooring of the hall—ere Bradfield rose. 'How fortunate! Not before him, however. What an idea!' He then rang the bell.

'Order a fire to be lighted immediately in the little room at the end of the passage; I have some business to transact; and see that I am not disturbed.'

His orders were instantly obeyed. In less than half-an-hour he began a search in the same chamber in which we have seen Dan Morton pursuing the same occupation. It was not with the same result. First he looked for the keys, destroying three or four memoranda, and consigning them to the fire; then he searched the iron safes and boxes, but he knew as well as most men that there was nothing there. But he had suddenly recollected that, in this room, his father had passed much of his time, and that here Giles Morton had been employed in putting up the mantel-piece, and in superintending the arrangements of the room. Bit by bit the whole thing came upon his recollection. This table was old Morton's work; the chair on which he sat was the old man's suggestion and manufacture. How could he have been so shortsighted? Thank goodness Darville was gone, and now he could have it all to himself.

He then began to examine the room: the wainscoat, the shutters, the closed drawers of an escritoir; but his search was unsuccessful. He turned to the mantel-piece: he examined the carving, he tapped the panels. Ah! what is that? As he looked at the square centre his hair grew cold, and that ominous beating of the heart began. He looked closely at it. What? It has been tampered with: lately, too. The place where it had been closed had been lately moved. He presses it sharply—it yields immediately to his touch, and, as the panel slides back, he discovers an empty space

He is sick at heart—sicker than Dan Morton, when he first saw the empty safe—and fell back, for this is his last chance. The paper has been there, and is there no more! Can it be destroyed? No! for the evidence of his own senses shows that something has been taken thence. By whom? That's a fearful question for Abel Bradfield to answer. Is he surrounded by spies? Who are his servants? Do they know anything about this? How should they? Is it his son?

It seemed to Abel Bradfield that that paper, in the hands of Laurence, would be sure to reach its destination. He knew his son too well to think that he would have hesitated a day: that was the only gleam of sunshine that visited him in his darkness. Yes; there were but two people who could have had access to it, in any way interested—Hugh Darville and Laurence Bradfield. The former? Impossible! The latter? Improbable! Besides which, he knew well that his first impulse would be to bring it to him—to his father. Yet they distrusted one another, and he might have taken it elsewhere. However, it must have gone one way or the other, whoever had it, to himself or to Sir Michael Carrington. He had heard nothing of it yet. Could it be a myth altogether! Inaction was worse than death. He was compelled to hope for the best and to suffer the worst, and so we must leave him for the present.

CHAPTER V.

SILVERMERE.

'Er muss reisen, aber zein Herz bleibt zurück.'
KOTZEBUE.

LONDON was not yet full, but the clubs were. Business had brought the men to the metropolis, now that hunting was almost over. A few packs, with fine woodlands, or in wet or not very forward countries, were having a few more last days, and a monomaniac or two stuck to them still; but the majority had changed their quarters; and Limmer's, and Long's, the Clarendon and Stevens', the Arlington, the Reform, the Conservative, Boodle's, Brookes', and White's, gave evidence of the migratory nature of the English gentleman.

On the steps of one of the principal political clubs of London stood half-a-dozen men of various ages discussing the debate of the previous evening.

'What do you say, Milham?' asked Lord Gossamer.

'The most promising young one out, my lord.'

'A trifle heavy; not prosaic exactly, but bookish,' rejoined his lordship.

'Requirements of the age, my lord. No use now to talk about what one doesn't understand. Time's rather valuable, and the country has found it out. Besides, education is a toughish subject; not like any of your light questions—a continental war, or Schleswig and Holstein.'

'Very eloquent; at least he was listened to very attentively for three quarters of an hour.'

'Plenty of sense, as well as sound. That's what people like now. The speech reads as well as it sounded. Depend upon it there has not been a better maiden attempt these five years,' said Admiral Downright.

'Rising young man,' said Tom Dunderfield, who had been one himself the last five-and-twenty years, and always acknowledged, but hated rivals.

'Rising,' said Milham, 'you mean risen. Upon my soul it was the most refreshing thing we've had this session. It was delightful to see the way in which he overhauled Thwackham's theories, and separated the chaff from the wheat. He put us all in the hole—his own party as well as ours.'

'What do you call his party?'

'Why, he sat on the Liberal benches and talked conservatism—that is, it looked liked conservatism trying to find its way out of the surrounding darkness by the light of liberality. He'll soon have a party of his own, if he makes many more such speeches as that.'

'But he calls himself Liberal.'

'His father takes the trouble off his hands in that respect, though he declined to stand for his county on the Liberal interest,' said Milham.

That's because he would not oppose the Carrington interest.'

'Considerate of him,' said Dunderfield; 'have the women nothing to do with it?'

'Women? I should think not—what can they have to do with it?' asked Milham, who never saw anything beyond his nose, and that imperfectly.

'Oh! nothing, of course,' rejoined the other, 'I merely asked the question; don't say I said anything about it, only they do say he's confoundedly attentive to Evelyn Carrington; and certainly the old iron-master's money might not come amiss in that quarter. Two generations of Carringtons are about equal to a general war.'

At that moment Laurence Bradfield appeared on the steps, and the coterie separated, looking at one another unutterable things.

'Hallo! Bradfield, where are you going?' said Carrington, who crossed Pall Mall at that moment, and thought of nothing better to say.

'I'm on way to Mentmore's; but I must call at Sommerton on my road, as I have to take down my mother and sister to-morrow. I shall endeavour to stay for the recess.'

Stafford Carrington manifested greater interest in his proceedings, and asked him 'by what train he intended to go?'

'By the 3.30 P.M. Saxonby to-morrow; it will get us down in time for dinner.'

'I'm very glad to hear we shall meet. We are going down to-morrow too, probably at the same time.'

The young men parted, both in excellent humour with the other, and neither willing to admit the reason why. Evangeli!—the messengers of good-tidings are always welcome.

The most beautiful place in the county of —— is Silvermere. It has belonged to the Mentmore family since the wars of the Roses, at which time it came into their hands in exchange for an estate which had been forfeited during an opposition occupancy of the throne in those troublous times. The house was large, roomy, and commodious, without one architectural beauty. It partook of all styles, and had enjoyed apparently the worst epoch of each; and yet, from its situation alone, it was never regarded than as one of the lions of the county. It was placed half-way down an amphitheatre of magnificent woodland hills. On three sides the most luxuriant foliage alternated with abruptly terminating hills. Here and there a vista was opened to a distant prospect, disclosing the blue outline of another country. Three sides of the house itself were backed by noble trees, at a sufficient distance to relieve it from dampness; and notwithstanding its architectural deficiencies, it stood out from its dark-green background a noble mass of warm-coloured stone. The turrets at either corner were adorned with flags during the residence of the family, and marked to the neighbourhood a season of hospitality and cheerfulness, which had made it famous from generation to generation.

It was approached on all sides by fine roads, showing the taste and munificence of its owner, as you came nearer the property. For a mile or two around, before entering on the domain, the roads and hedges were trimmer, the little villages and school-houses neater, the sides of the ways were kept with more scrupulous care and attention. The very children and old dames looked brighter and cleaner, as they curtsied to the occupants of one of the castle carriages, or a fly evidently bearing its freight to that all-powerful mansion. Once within any of the numerous lodge-gates which surrounded the home-park, and the traveller had come upon a garden. Each side of the well-gravelled drives was mown like a lawn for some ten or twelve feet back, till the mossy turf lost itself gradually in the shrubs and among the bolls of the magnificent trees, on which might be seen and heard the shy wood-pigeon; while below ran constantly across the road the pheasant and the rabbit, more in wanton gambols than in fear. At intervals along the green turf were planted the finest of our hardy shrubs, and choice Americans, azalias, and rhododendrons; and the feathery branches of the deodara, the araucaria, and the Wellingtonia swept the ground. Here and there a rustic temple, or the porch of some secluded keeper's cottage, drooping with creepers, just beginning to bloom again, gave a look of homely comfort to this Arcadian scene; and a bubbling fountain invited the stranger to linger yet, before he terminated the enchantment of nature by the tamer enjoyments of artificial life.

Approaching the house the woods widen, and are thrown back into large open glades, displaying a park, in which deer may be seen herding together, and the long-haired black north-country cattle grazing in all directions. On the right lies the beautiful piece of water, from which the place has taken its name. Its shores are studded with boats, punts, and all the adjuncts for pleasure parties and sport. On the left a broad and gently-sloping road, of the finest gravel, leads up to the principal entrance to the house, which recedes between two projecting wings. On the one side lie the offices, and on the other lie rooms less frequently in use, excepting when (as on the present occasion) an influx of company brings them into occupation. The large reception rooms lead from the hall, and with the exception of the billiard-room, look upon the other side of the house.

But the grand feature of Silvermere still remains to be portrayed. The fourth side looks, unimpeded by trees or hills, along a lovely vale as far as the eye can reach. A river's silvery stream winds rapidly but smoothly through it, forming here and there larger reservoirs of water, as the beauty of the landscape may seem to have required. Immediately in front of this side of the house is the flower-garden,—a garden not only unequalled in England, but in any part of the known world It is what is usually known as a lawn, but of such vast and inconceivable dimensions, that the word conveys no sort of idea of the reality. It is a lawn in its luxuriant and mossy turf, in its perfect order and beauty, in its perfection of detail. It is a park in its size, in the undulations of its ground, in the magnificent grouping of its finest trees; some of which in their untamed luxuriance have grown downwards and again taken root upwards, forming from their single stems whole masses of foliage, and showing suckers larger than the parent stem. Here in every variety may be seen the most magnificent and costly firs, cedars, and pines; art and munificence supplying the deficiencies of our colder clime. Large and well-arranged conservatories exhibit the most rare and costly exotics; and are so built and placed as to give a fairy-like lightness to their size and extent. Here and there, one above the other, are basins, on whose bosoms are erected fountains from the finest models, and which throw their waters hundreds of feet high, colouring the landscape to the eye as it looks through the dropping spray. When summer brings her flowers to perfection, huge masses of the most brilliant colour may be seen with scarcely an intervening space of green in some places, whilst in the further distance, and over the hilly sides of the lawn, along the slopes, and through the scattered foliage of the shrubs and trees, the eye may trace a ribbon-border of the brightest flowers stretching away to the utmost limits of the lawn. Silvermere, in a word, was one of the loveliest spots in existence; it had neither a rival nor a mistress.

Before Laurence Bradfield and his mother and sister started on their proposed visit, two things occurred which we must not pass over.

It will be in the recollection of the reader that when Laurence had his struggle with Dan Morton in the plantation, the only trophy which he brought away with him was a leaded stick. It was nowise remarkable, and looked at first sight equally capable of knocking on the head a man or a pheasant. On closer inspection, however, it proved to be so.

Miss Bradfield had a dog, a water-spaniel and retriever; as a favourite he was occasionally to be found in all parts of the house. One evening as they were sitting after dinner, in the temporary absence of Mr. Bradfield, Sambo entered the dining-room, bringing with him the stick in question. He laid it down with much grace by the side of his mistress.

'What has the dog there, Ellen?' said Laurence.

'A stick, dear; he brought it out of my room, I suppose. It has been there some time.'

'Just let me look at it—thank you; I know it,' and he smiled quietly. 'Curious wood, is it not? very heavy—I forget the name of it—but I know it is Australian.'

'Australian: is it? Nanny Fletcher says it belongs to Dan Morton.'

'And who is Dan Morton, Ellen?' said her brother, with some animation.

'A great big fellow, who lives by poaching and other respectable means. He professes to be a tenant of papa's, and to work at the iron-works; but I never heard of his doing anything.'

'Then Mr. Dan Morton is the gentleman whom I caught poaching or love-making here one night. Capital stick, isn't it?' and here Laurence Bradfield surveyed his prize complacently,—'handsome wood.'

'Of course, I remember, she told me that he had been years in Australia. He had to leave the country for something or other, not very creditable.'

'Precisely—he must be the person. And where is he now?'

'Oh! I haven't the slightest idea. I scarcely know him; but it's an old Sommerton name.'

Laurence appeared to meditate a few moments, then his face resumed its ordinary serenity; and picking up the stick he stood by the door while his mother and sister retired.

Ladies'-maids are of delicate materials; still they find a limit to their ailments, when their mistresses exhibit an antipathy to chronic ill-health. The consequence was the speedy recovery of Ellen's maid, and the return to her house of Nancy Fletcher. Thus it came to pass that the piece of paper which Scarsdale had dropt, and which Job Fletcher had carried to his wife, still remained in her possession; and though it excited her curiosity, it can hardly be said to have much perplexed her. After some time, however, spent in conjecture, as it contained the names of two families with whom she had some sort of connection, and seeing no other way of setting her doubts at rest, she determined upon taking the paper to Miss Ellen, as she was called in the village.

Miss Ellen was rather puzzled at the circumstance; and not having much idea of business, very naturally postponed entering on the subject until she should see her brother. Laurence, however, was not to be caught during the session at all times; and thus the note which old Morton had given to Mr. Scarsdale passed about two or three months in the hands of Mrs. Job Fletcher, and the same time in those of Ellen Bradfield. Knowing but indistinctly the relations which had existed between the Bradfields and Carringtons, she had put it away, and when chance brought it to light she felt very little interest in an old and time-honoured memorandum. She did however much the same to resolve her doubts as Nanny had done before to her. She presented the paper to Mr. Scarsdale.

'Bless me, Miss Bradfield! and where did you get this?'

'Nanny Fletcher gave it to me. She knows nothing about it; no more do I.'

'And why did you give it to me?'

'Because you are the great "medicine man" of the village; and if it is of no use to you, I'm sure nobody else knows what to do with it. I was going to destroy it.'

'But it belongs to me.'

'Belongs to you; does it? Then I wish you joy of so valuable a possession.'

'I must have dropped it in the village. Good morning, Miss Bradfield.'

'He's a very curious person is Mr. Scarsdale. I never used to think him uncertain, but he is very much altered these last three months. My poor father frets him, I presume; but that's no reason he should be so very odd in his manner to me.'

Ellen Bradfield was not in love, or she might have been odd herself.

Scarsdale had recovered his lost note, and was not much nearer the end of his skein for that. He had only been reminded that if Sir Reginald Carrington would go to Patcham and pay some money, he would receive the release. Heads or tails! there was not much to be got out of that.

'Hallo!' shouted Captain Trumps, with his mouth full of *cotelette aux points d'asperge*, and rushing to the window, 'here's a row, Lady Mary.' Lady Mary deserted her egg; and a very pretty couple they looked as they stood, framed and glazed, staring into the garden. 'Look at the people: there's something wrong. Be Jove, they're all coming towards the house.'

Lady Mary applied her glass to her eye, and beheld the advance of apparently hostile troops from all quarters, over-running the whole gardens, sauntering here, there, and everywhere, stopping to admire the views, or to take up a position, looking up at the trees, and speculating on them as a catapult for forcing the doors. 'Dear me, Captain Trumps, what is to be done? And what a set! did you ever! they look like operatives.'

'By Jove, this is the great unwashed; some beastly attack on the aristocracy,' said Trumps, who was rather amused with the proceeding, and who smoothed down his black, glossy, crimpled curls, for which he was remarkable among his brother officers. 'Lots of women too; and there's one with a baby. They don't go on to the grass, that's one thing; Mentmore's deuced fond of his grass, Lady Mary.'

'But, dear me, Captain Trumps. Why don't you ring the bell; surely the house is going to be put into a state of defence—pray ring the bell.'

'Oh! certainly, if you wish it;' and Trumps went to the bell. Everybody else had finished breakfast an hour ago. Trumps and Lady Mary were always late, from some curious coincidence, which neither of them could explain. Having rung the bell, he resumed his place at the window, and burst out laughing. 'Oh! I know what it is now. These are the people from Coppernails; it's a town about six miles off; it's a great fighting place, and Mentmore has lent them the park. Most good-natured fellow, Mentmore. I suppose they've mistaken the way.'

Lady Mary was not an admirer of the Prize Ring, so she said, 'Lent them the park! oh! nonsense, Captain Trumps; how could he lend them the park? He's a magistrate, and a legislator and all that sort of thing.'

'Oh!' said Trumps, laughing heartily, 'magistrates and legislators like fights, and wouldn't put a stop to them for the world. It's only the police. Those fellows are always in the way, except when they're wanted. Oh! oh! I say, Mr. Stubbs, there's a lot of people all over the gardens; hadn't you better tell Lord Mentmore as soon as possible?'

'Yes, and get the front door closed and

barred,' added Lady Mary, 'as soon as possible.' Mr. Stubbs made his way to the window.

'Oh! my lady, you needn't be afraid, my lady. It's only the people from Coppernails. My lord allows them to come every Monday, Wednesday, and Friday; we have a thousand or more sometimes in the summer; they bring their perwisions, my lady.'

'What, then, are we confined to the billiard room, or the open country for the day?' asked Captain Trumps. 'I vote we go for a ride, Lady Mary.'

'Oh no, sir, certainly not. There's my lord, and Mr. Bradfield, and the duchess, and Miss Bradfield, and Mr. Carrington, and most of the gentlemen, have been out there this half-hour. Would you take a little more tea, my lady?'

'No, thank you, Mr. Stubbs.'

'Just bring me those cutlets, Stubbs, if they're hot. Thank you, that will do,' said the captain, helping himself; 'the cream, please, that will do;' and Mr. Stubbs left the room, while Lady Mary resumed her seat.

'That's so like Mentmore, isn't it? I do think he's the kindest creature in the whole world,' remarked her ladyship, who having partly given up Mentmore as a bad job after three seasons, still had the good sense and honesty to praise him. Trumps felt a little aggrieved.

'I thought Mentmore was by way of being a tremendous Tory?'

'So he is, I believe; that is, he voted with dear papa last session, on the censure of ministers; but he has very liberal notions on some points.'

'And this is one of them.'

'Well, now! I declare I like him all the better for it,' said the lady; 'he always thinks for himself, pa says; and that's something.'

'Yes! I think he is a capital fellow; but this is entirely Bradfield's doing; he has become uncommonly thick there lately. What do you think of the girl?' This was rather a sharp thrust from the captain; as it was currently reported that Mentmore was turning his thoughts that way.

At that moment he entered the room. 'Oh! Lady Mary, I am ashamed of you; we finished breakfast an hour ago; but I hope you have everything you want; if not, Trumps will be so good as to ring for Mr. Stubbs.'

'Lord Mentmore, is it true that you have these people here all over the gardens, three days a week?'

'Indeed I do, Lady Mary. I hope it meets with your approbation.'

'Oh that's so charming. It is so delightful to see them about, with their dear little babies, and hard-boiled eggs, and that sort of thing, you know. It's so good-natured of you, too, for they must do a great deal of mischief.'

'None that is not set right in a day,' said his lordship.

'But they pick the flowers and break the shrubs.'

'Very seldom indeed; besides a flower or two would not ruin us here, though it is strictly prohibited,' as you may see in the grounds. They're very well-behaved, good sort of people, and work very hard at times; an outing, as they call it, does them good.'

'I'll tell you what, Mentmore, you ought to return your own man for Coppernails—there's no mistake about that.'

'Perhaps I do,' said he, laughing; 'would you like to sit for it, Trumps; is that the sort of constituency you'd like to shake hands with?'

'I'd rather do it after they were washed,' said Trumps, turning his ring round, and looking at his own neat, well-shaped, and well-coloured fingers.

'You're fastidious. Bradfield does not care a straw about it. He says there's more dirt done by clean hands, than by grimy ones, sometimes.'

'That's your new friend, Lord Mentmore,' said Lady Mary. 'He's charming, quite. I do delight in originality.'

'Then come out into the gardens; you'll see plenty of it. Come along, Trumps, if you're going to stand for Coppernails, you must get some knowledge of your constituency. I'll introduce you;' and they all went out to look at the people, who were already, thus early in the day, scattered over the pleasure-grounds; admiring the views, or the flowers, or lounging by the cool-looking reservoirs, waiting for the playing of the fountains, which had been promised them.

One of the circumstances connected with Mentmore's popularity, was his regard for other people. It was not that he was not selfish; any man brought up as he had been, must have become so, more or less; but he made certain self-sacrifices to the masses, which showed rather sympathy with classes than with individuals. It is a higher excellence of the same virtue. Sympathy with individuals is often prompted by personal liking; sympathy with the multitude, never. The *civis Romanus* was a greater man in the integrity of his character than Pylades or Orestes. The greatest security for success in life, is a genial sympathy with other people. When a man wants this, he may be a good friend and an excellent man, but he can never be a popular one.

The greatest boon that had ever been granted to the poor of Coppernails was this rural treat. Overworked, sometimes half-fed, they still strove for an occasional holiday as far as Silvermere. If a man had only bread to eat, he could here eat it with his wife and children, surrounded by luxuries of nature which few could enjoy. Monday is a proverbially idle day among the factory people. Whole van-loads in the fine spring and summer weather might be met between the two places; to be counted always in hundreds, upon great occasions by thousands. But it was something more than this. The people began to attach an importance to this permission which it did not carry with it. They regarded the owner of Silvermere as a personal protector. It seemed to them as if nothing could go quite wrong while they participated in such splendour. They came to attach some of his greatness to themselves; and many a heart-ache has been cured or postponed by the unpretending and natural thoughtfulness of Lord Mentmore.

On the present occasion the groups which filled the grounds appeared to be actuated by a delicacy not commonly attributed to English people. There was an evident wish not to intrude upon the company at the castle; and a great portion of the garden nearest to the house was thus unoccupied excepting by the guests or the family. Lady Mary, aided by Captain Trumps and Lord Mentmore, became wonderfully bold, and was soon amusing herself with the peculiarities of that class of the people of which she knew least. Trumps was quite at home; and called his companions' attention to the beauty often met with among the class of operatives. If less healthful than that of peasant life, it is frequently more delicate, and approaches more nearly to an educated standard of excellence.

Just then a shout arose, which faintly spread through the grounds, and a concourse of people ran towards the water, as the fountains began to play. In a few seconds they were throwing their jets high in the air, and the people were amusing themselves as the spray, borne by the light breeze, began wetting the women and children who stood nearest to the water's edge. A little incident took place which attracted attention to a man who might otherwise have escaped remark, unless it had been given to his fine proportions and handsome face. On the upper side of the highest basin stood Lord Mentmore, the Duchess of Caradoc, Lady Mary Gwendolyn, Miss Carrington, and Mrs. Bradfield, with a few of the hardiest spirits, anxious to obtain a closer inspection of the duchess and her bonnet. For the benefit of the reader we may mention that it was of grey crape and point lace.

Lower down stood Stafford Carrington, Ellen Bradfield, and her brother; three or four men, who were the devoted slaves of any pretty woman for the time being, and our friend Trumps, who amused himself with backing one gold fish against the other, with the colonel, for half-a-crown a mile, as he called a stipulated distance marked by a stick at the bottom of the pool. When the spray fell on the tidy bonnets and shawls of the excursionists, there was a little push to get out of the way. In the *mêlée* a young and delicate woman, who held a child of some weight in her arms, was pushed so near the edge of the basin, which was undefended, that she fell over the side, and she and her child were straightway immersed in the water. It was deep enough to have drowned the baby, and as the poor woman raised herself, so she seemed to think, by her appeal for help. At that moment a handsome-looking fellow in a shooting jacket, with fine dark eyes and hair, and remarkable in the crowd by his height and figure, walked off the stone edging up to his waist, and seizing the child as it lay a bundle of screaming clothes, about to sink, handed it to a bystander as huge and strong as himself, and as ugly as the other was handsome. Having then tenderly wiped its little face and hands, which were none the worse for the washing, he handed it to its mother.

The incident had not escaped notice, of course, and Lord Mentmore sent a gardener to have the woman and the child taken to one of the lodges. When he went down to look for the man, thinking his wetting should be rewarded by a sovereign, he and his friend were nowhere to be found.

'Do you see the man's face, who picked the child out of the water, Ellen? I know it quite well, but cannot recollect who it is. Here, come nearer; there he goes, with that great big fellow; he looks very little like a Copper-nails man.'

'Yes! I know him well enough. What can he be doing here? It's Job Fletcher, Laurence.'

'So it is, Miss Bradfield: what capital eyes you have; and that's the greatest poacher in the country with him, that big fellow. His name's Morton. He's been up before my father often enough.'

'The other's a Sommerton man, Mr. Carrington. I should have thought you hardly took sufficient interest in our village to have known anything about him.'

'You know he married a sort of maid and *protégée* of my great-aunt, so that we have some sort of acquaintance with him. Besides which I feel an interest in many things that I get very little credit for, Miss Bradfield, and Sommerton is one of them.'

Ellen Bradfield distributed the leaves of a rose rather deliberately on the grass, and was suddenly seized with an anxious desire to know what Captain Trumps was about.

'Trumps, Miss Bradfield? Just now he is torturing goldfish with his riding-whip. Curious how naturally cruel we all are.'

'Inconsiderate, I think you mean; and men more than women.'

'Perhaps that's the right word; the result, however, is the same. But I am not prepared to subscribe to the last theory, by any means. Indeed, I think the reverse is the case.'

'Why, Mr. Carrington,' said the young lady, opening her eyes, 'you forget all your sports: the foxes, the birds, the fish, to say nothing of the infant recreations of birds-nesting, ant-destroying, cockchafer-spinning, daddy-long-legs-mutilating, and all the other juvenile amusements of the male population.'

'Truly you seem remarkably well-up in the sports of childhood, as well as manhood; but you know there are theorists who vow that foxes like being hunted, and horses ridden after them. To be sure, we never suspect young ladies of catching flies, or spinning cockchafers, but they are supposed to have methods of their own for torturing their enemies; and what makes their cruelty the more wanton—it is said their friends.'

'Oh! that is a charge quite unintelligible; let us have an instance?'

'Here comes one—Trumps. He is a miserable example of the cruelty of Lady Mary Gwendolyn.'

'Now I understand, Mr. Carrington. Allow

me to say that she should be regarded rather as a general practitioner, with an interesting case on hand. The remedy is entirely in his own hands, or Lady Mary is only acting as the Nemesis of coquetry. Captain Trumps is a very feeble illustration of your doctrine.'

The gallant officer was just advancing.

'Well, Trumps, what have you been doing?' said Lord Mentmore, who had just joined them.

'I've been doing the colonel out of three half-crowns. He laid me three to one on one of the fish, while they were running; and just at the finish I came with a rush, and won on the post by a short head. I think it was that last scientific touch under the ribs that did it though.'

'Oh! that's your idea of a *finish*, is it?'

'If that's your idea of a pun, Mentmore, permit me to say that the colonel beats you into fits. When the match between us was first proposed, he thought we might both go *to scale*.'

The colonel, being like many other colonels,

not in the habit of electrifying his auditors by his wit, received a disproportionate ovation in his absence.

'What do you propose to do to-day, after luncheon, Lord Mentmore?' said the charming Duchess of Caradoc—charming in spite of her high birth, large fortune, and good looks, things which are supposed by some writers to militate against true virtue or goodness.

'I propose that we should visit the ruins of Silverstone—for there is a Silverstone as well as a Silvermere. Now, duchess, you shall do me the favour to chaperon Miss Bradfield, and I will accompany you, as I know all the points of interest. Lady Mary shall change places, and go with Mrs. Bradfield, and Captain Trumps shall be their escort; he knows all the country, and has amusing legends to tell of all the brooks, and many of the fences in it. Then, Bradfield, how will you go?'

'If you will lend me the pony I rode yesterday—'

'Oh! stay; we must provide for Lady and

Miss Carrington. Stafford, you ride; or do you prefer the phaëton?'

'Oh! pray don't have out a hack for me,' said Laurence Bradfield, suddenly changing his mind, as to the eligibility of riding; 'I really should be most happy to escort Lady Carrington, if she will allow me.'

'I prefer driving, Mentmore, I assure you; and if I don't inconvenience you, and the duchess—,' said Stafford Carrington—

'Inconvenience?' said the duchess, with her blandest smile. 'when was Mr. Carrington known to inconvenience anybody by his company?' It was so true that he might have done so by his absence, that to any impartial observer the change of countenance upon this rearrangement of parties, in at least four instances, would have been eminently apparent.

'So much for us,' said Mentmore; 'but what's to be done with Lord Dallington, and the colonel, and Stapleton, and Wilfred Jones, and three or four more. My aunt won't go; she never goes out with a party, sight-seeing. I think we'll give them the break; they're all men, and can smoke and do as they like. Dallington and Wilfred Jones are sure to handicap half the horses in Newmarket before they get back.'

The ruins were probably a great imposition—I know they generally are—but the ride answered its purpose. Mentmore lionized the duchess, as in duty bound, and Ellen Bradfield fell to Stafford Carrington's share.

Mentmore was scarcely satisfied with the arrangement—man is sometimes as changeable as woman. Once he had desired, above all things, that his friend Carrington should be more intimate with the Bradfields, and was disappointed that it was not so. His own accident had led to the fulfilment of his wishes; and now he almost regretted its results. The truth is, he was beginning to feel a renewal of that interest in Ellen Bradfield, which he had already experienced when a guest at her father's house. He was in a different situation here. Other ladies demanded his services, and, as a host, their demands were to be complied with. Even so, he would have preferred a less good-looking and attractive substitute than Stafford Carrington to take his place by Miss Bradfield's side.

'What did you think of the ruins, Bradfield?'

'Dam old,' said Wilfred Jones, who had not much idea of antiquity, excepting by the mouth. 'Couldn't do much in the way of making a house; too old to breed from, I should say.'

'The situation is considered very fine,' continued Lord Mentmore, not paying much attention to Wilfred Jones, except on the subject of racing.

'So it is. In themselves not so picturesque as some; they are in too good preservation. Some Dowager Lady Mentmore's house, I presume?'

'Yes; that's exactly what they are. And what will you fellows do now?'

'I'm going down to the cricket-ground;' 'So am I;' 'And I.' 'I must write letters,' said

Bradfield. 'As you like, I'll come shortly,' said Mentmore. 'You'll find Carrington, and Miss Carrington, and some of the ladies, down there now.'

Bradfield's letters were very short that afternoon.

CHAPTER VI.

AN AMBUSCADE.

'Illi alternantes multâ vi prælia miscent
Vulneribus crebris.'—VIRG.: *Georg.*, lib. iii.

I LIKE a cigar; and if intoxicating liquors have been obtained from different plants producing however a like effect, the same cannot be said for the narcotics in which we indulge. Each contains its own peculiar principle. I have no desire to rank with the opium-eater. The hop produces gout, notwithstanding its adherents over every country in which Englishmen have set foot. Strychnia, its occasional substitute, has peculiarly unpleasant results. The poppy and the lettuce are said to soothe pain and induce sleep; and a decoction of the former in use in Persia produces such marvellous effects upon the brain, that the most fulsome compliments follow the most violent quarrels and abuse.

But no such results spring from the moderate use of tobacco. If men could only be persuaded that pipes are for the vulgar, and, however fragrant, cannot but lower the true gentleman in his own estimation, we might still enjoy our national narcotic without a murmur. 'Those nasty pipes,' says Mrs. Smythe; 'not that I object to a cigar, my dear. I'm told the Duke of Cambridge, and even the Prince of Wales, occasionally indulge in such a luxury.' Of course! When the troubles or excitements (for there are men, whatever philosophers say, who have troubles, as Banting *par exemple*) of the day are over, when a really unexceptionable dinner has been tempered by a moderate use of the very best vintages, can anything be more delightful than that one well-made, well-conditioned cigar. None of your delicate, lady-like cigarettes for me, the very rolling up of which produces a feeling akin to medicinal treatment, but a fine full-flavoured regalia redolent of the south-western hemisphere, allaying all irritation, and predisposing to a calm and imperturbable self-reliance, which treats all questions, from personal abuse to pecuniary loss (the two hardest things in life to bear), with a spirit of philosophic indifference. I have imbued even the females of my family with the same enlightened view of this theory (in my own case I may say practice), and I perhaps owe to it, in moderation, that happy temperament which has carried me through innumerable difficulties, and for which the author believes himself to be as remarkable as he is grateful.

Well! it seems that plenty of persons are of the same opinion too. All the men in Lord Mentmore's house smoked, excepting himself, and he did his best to encourage it, by supplying the cigars. I don't know who was his man, Hudson, Carlin, Goode, or whether he imported them, as some men do their wit, from a native manufactory, but they were first-rate. The consequence was unmitigated patronage by

Dallington, Trumps, the Colonel, Carrington, Stapleton, Wilfred Jones, and Bradfield, whose parliamentary duties seemed to involve him in a round of dissipation, entirely foreign to the sedate and sedentary habits of his former university life. A good fellow and a good man is often a different being; in Bradfield the two had found a home.

'What does Lord Ovenham think of his horse for the guineas, Trumps—have you ever heard him say?'

'If he thinks half as much of his horse as he does of himself, he must have tolerable hedging even at his present price; and it's not a very short one,' replied Mr. Trumps, whose opinion of Lord Ovenham did not tally with that young nobleman's own estimate of his advantages.

'But have you ever heard him say anything about it?'

'No, I haven't, nor anybody else either. He never mentions him for two reasons.'

'What are they?' The room seemed interested in the reply.

'First of all he doesn't know how to pronounce his name quite properly; and secondly, he's afraid of Wilfred Jones getting the information.'

'Trumps has eaten something that has disagreed with him,' said Stafford Carrington, 'he is a complete *mauvaise langue* to-night. Mentmore stands a whole pot of money on his horse, doesn't he?' This question was addressed to Wilfred Jones, who replied by puffing slowly out a volume of smoke, and looking as if he had not heard a word.

'The horse ought to win; he did a good thing with Agricola at even weights yesterday,' said Lord Dallington. Still Wilfred Jones smoked on.

'Won his trial with seven pounds in hand, it makes the guineas quite safe, and he'll be first favourite for the Derby. I hope all you fellows have got your money on; they only bid me seven and eight to one at the corner yesterday;' saying which Mr. Trumps, Lieutenant and Captain, uncorked a bottle of seltzer water, and poured it on the top of some sherry.

'I took fifteen ponies in the winter,' said Carrington, 'the only bet I have on the race.'

'It's a good bet now, Carrington,' said Wilfred Jones, at last.

'I feel inclined to stand it—I suppose the horse is sure to win?'

'He's a very good horse, and bred to stay. Idolatry would stay for ever;' and here the master of the horse having satisfied prejudice, and told nothing that was not well known before, relapsed into silence and enfolded himself in smoke.

'What a good-natured thing it is of Mentmore to have all those people in the gardens,' said Laurence Bradfield; 'he says they do no harm.'

'I thought that was what you fellows go for; Lady Mary says it's the liberal dodge to go for the manufacturing interests,' said Trumps.

'I don't think Mentmore cares more for the manufacturing interests than any other. There seemed to me to be some people there who certainly hadn't much to do with Coppernails.'

And while the rest of the company amused themselves with divers subjects, I may as well give a sketch of our friend Wilfred Jones.

The enormous increase in the size of studs had created a want. Formerly noblemen or gentlemen were considered capable of managing their own racing establishments. They were no longer so; and it became necessary to select a friend or acquaintance of equal capacity, but less means, to overlook the training, entering, and general care of the horses. It was not an uncommon thing for a man to place his property and his honour in the hands of a Master of the Horse. This was precisely the case with Mentmore. With a colossal fortune, but without time to enjoy more than a twentieth part of it, his princely munificence was equal to the support of anything. Over his racing establishment he placed, with proconsular power, one Wilfred Jones.

What were his antecedents? I propose to give them as the type of a rather numerous class of the present day. It will not occupy a minute.

Wilfred Jones was a cornet in a cavalry regiment. As a boy at school he had been remarkable for keeping his place without ever indulging in the luxury of a book, or a verse task; and he had the peculiarity of being always, even as a youngster, the companion of bigger boys. This characteristic had stuck to him through life. It could never be ascertained that he had any money, but he maintained his position in society by spending four thousand a year; and though socially a lower-form boy he was always to be found among bigger men. He had graduated at Eton, and in the —— Hussars; was capital company; lived entirely upon the turf; numbered a certain Lady Jones among his relatives; spoke of his *gens* (our people he called them) as of undoubted respectability; and, whenever he was missed from the great clubs, Long's, Limmer's, or the

Arlington, was supposed to be staying with an aunt in Bryanstone Square.

In appearance he was well-made, well-dressed, and gentlemanly-looking; accustomed to the usages of good society, speaking but one language, and that questionably, more from habit than education. Strictly honourable, though the world scarcely believed it; good-humoured, well-disposed, a friend to all men, and a great favourite with fast women; pre-eminently a non-marrying man. In a word, Wilfred Jones had the misfortune to be born with the tastes of fifteen thousand a year, and with just three hundred to gratify them.

At this moment, Mentmore, to the surprise of everyone, opened the door.

'Who's for an expedition?'

'What's the row?' asked Trumps.

'Sackham, the keeper, has been here, and he says there's some poaching to be done to-night in the Home wood. Who would like to come?'

The volunteers rose as a man. 'Trumps,

as a military swell, had better have the post of danger,' said Dallington.

'Certainly!' said Trumps, who, to do him justice, looked as eager for the fray as anyone; 'but just explain, that's a good fellow.'

'Well, then, at this time of year there's a great trade in pheasants' eggs; and poachers in a place like this are as thick as thieves upon the ground.'

'Precisely; and if I understand rightly, Mr. Sackham wants an auxiliary force, as he expects rather more trouble than usual.'

'Look here; we have had information that the poachers here have been reinforced by a part of a strange gang; and as it really is of great consequence to have the eggs just now, as I don't approve of buying them unless I know where they come from; Mr. Sackham wants to organize a force sufficient to catch these fellows, and he thinks he can do it to-night. The moon will be up in about an hour; so we've no time to lose.'

'Nothing more charming,' said one. 'I'll

just change these things of mine,' said another. 'Give me a glass of that sherry,' said a third. A fourth inquired whether Sackham provided sticks, which he did; and a fifth borrowed a pair of shooting boots and gaiters of Mentmore's valet, having nothing but thin boots and shoes with him; Carrington inquired for a pea-jacket, as it was cold, and some vesuvians; and Bradfield rolled himself from his arm-chair slowly but determinedly, as he said to Carrington, 'Now we shall catch that infernal rascal we saw in the morning, with my sister's good-looking friend, Mr. Job Fletcher, or I'm very much mistaken.'

Mr. Sackham stood outside with a strong army of under-keepers; it is just possible that he might have turned out with a whole body of villagers to surround the woods, or to beat them as on a battue day; but the lateness of the intelligence prevented any premeditation. He was compelled to use the materials which presented themselves, and we are bound to speak well of their readiness and adaptability to the work. When he was joined by the amateur division, he would have been formidable under any circumstances; the presence of so much gentle blood made him doubly dangerous to his enemies.

'You don't mean to say these fellows show fight for the eggs, Sackham?' said Laurence Bradfield.

''Deed they do, sir; your poacher, 'specially them as comes from a distance, or one as has had his six months, be uncommon spiteful.' And Mr. Sackham clutched his small leaded stick, which he carried in his pocket.

'And what makes you think that these fellows come under that description?'

'I know last summer assizes the Chief Baron gave six months and hard labour to some of our men in hope of breaking up the gang, and he nearly succeeded, but there's a bad lot come over from Cambridgeshire. They hear all about my lord's birds and his shooting, at Newmarket, and there's a ready sale for eggs all over those parts; Suffolk's a great county for preserving, sir. The worst of it is, the gentlemen ain't particular enough; and some o' the keepers knows it's as much as their place is worth to be without birds; and then they will buy any quantity, as long as they don't come off their own grounds.'

'I suppose they often do?'

'Lor', bless ye, sir, many a time I've had eggs offered me, taken from here the night before; but my lord won't buy from the poachers; and now they've found that out, it's astonishing what little egg-stealing there is about these covers. It's all these blackguards from other parts; but we'll be even wi' 'em.'

The wood in question, and a small field near it, in which were a great many coops for the hatching out of eggs by hens, was some little distance from the castle, and on their way thither a quiet conversation of the kind above related took place more or less along the whole line, between Lord Mentmore's guests and his keepers. As they approached the scene of action, strict silence was ordered, and Mr.

Sackham proceeded to marshal his troops, with reference to the ground, and the object he had in view. Let us state these in a few words. The wood was tolerably large; in fact of such an acreage that escape was not difficult should the marauders get timely notice of the advent of the keepers and their assistants. It had been reconnoitred in the day-time by some of those who had taken advantage of the public day in the grounds, and the fact that a great number of nests were to be found in one particular part of the cover was now as well known to the poachers as to the watchers and keepers themselves. In the centre of the wood was a broad ride, used during the hunting season, as the principal road through the cover, then deep and holding as the nature of the soil necessitated, and now dry and full of deep holes and ruts, as clay is accustomed to become after the first winds of March followed by hot weather in April and May. It was, therefore, difficult to run in, even to an active man, and hopeless to anyone else. The thickest boots and the most lithesome ankles would have the best chance. At the top of this ride was a well-covered circular hill, and around this hill was the place most in request by the pheasants for laying. Little rippling streams ran down from springs in its sides, which formed convenient basins here and there for water, and altogether from the lighter nature of the soil, and facilities of food, it was more frequented than the rest of the wood. The ride before mentioned ran round the base of the hillock, making a gentle rise all round; and information had been given from a well-informed source that this was the key of the poachers' position, from which some hundreds of eggs might be obtained.

The object of Mr. Sackham was not to scare them; or a show of his real strength might easily have effected it. The safety of his pheasants, and that of his neighbours, rather depended upon capturing a sufficient number of these poachers to break up the gang; and as 'evil communications corrupt good manners,' to deter the weak and vain, by making an example of the evilly disposed. There is no crime in the world, perhaps, in which the gradations of vice are so marked as in poaching; and one reason why a very severe punishment for anything like open and daring assault, or a public defiance of legal strength and authority is desirable, is the hope that younger hands and less malicious offenders may be deterred from a career whose end is unseen, and whose results cannot be calculated. This by way of parenthesis.

'Now, gentlemen,' said Mr. Sackham, in an audible whisper, as the moon showed herself above the horizon, large and luminous, 'single file, if you please, in the shadow of this fence. It leads direct to the bottom of the cover. I'll tell you, gentlemen, which way to go when we get there. Sykes, go on, and lie down quietly within thirty yards of the gate at the end under the old gipsy's oak; and put Bill Thornton opposite, about the same distance. If they come in at the bottom, close into the edge of the ride, but don't let them hear or see you. If they run for it, they're sure to run that way, down the hill—we'll leave two or three of these gentlemen in the ditch by the gate to help, and you're sure to get some on 'em. When you close, blow your whistle; not before.' And on they marched in single file, as ordered; each grasping a weapon of defiance or attack, in divers costumes, as fancy or convenience had dictated: knickerbockers, jack-boots, thick shoes, and gaiters, and one or two improvident souls, with their black dress trousers tucked into their boots,—vain defence against brushwood and gorse, at least three feet high.

'Beg pardon, gentlemen, but there's somebody a smokin'; nothin' a poacher know better nor the smell o' bacca.'

Trumps and Carrington extinguished their cigars in silence. Before long they reached the corner of the wood, which here formed a right angle with the fence; and Mr. Sackham proceeded to make his final arrangements for netting the lot. They were somewhat as follows:—

Two men were deposited in a wet ditch, outside the cover, close to the gate, to assist Sykes and Bill Thornton in stopping the fugitives, should they take to the main ride for escape. Trumps and Lord Dallington occupied this place of honour. As smoking and talking were forbidden, they had time to calculate the chances of committing manslaughter, or being murdered; not exactly an 'even main chance.' Be that as it may, they promised great things, and were very likely persons to fulfil their promises. The rest were carried through narrow and unfrequented paths, with much mystery and quiet, parallel with the great ride, and posted at intervals of about one hundred yards, with orders to render assistance upwards, should Sackham blow his whistle, or cries of assistance reach them from the upper end, or to keep close and follow up the fugitives, should they be seen making for the gate at the bottom. The gentlemen thus placed at intervals, were faced on the other side by corresponding sentinels along the whole line. Wilfred Jones,

Stapleton, Laurence Bradfield, Carrington, and Lord Mentmore, with some more watchers, followed slowly towards the hill; and when there, were placed at intervals round its base, concealed by brushwood, bolls of trees, or loose boulders, which lay here and there on the slope the signs of some former operations of nature, more in the way of Lyell or Tindal to explain than in mine. Having thus laid a remarkably creditable ambuscade, Mr. Sackham betook himself to the rear of the hill, determined upon making his attack from behind, at which moment he was to be joined by the sharp-shooters in front. It was calculated that the sudden attack from all sides at once, would necessitate a surrender.

CHAPTER VII.

THE EGGS ARE SAVED, BUT NOT THE BACON.

'Wann man unter den Wölven ist muss man mit heulen.'

UNDER no circumstances whatever could the situation be called a pleasant one. To men who are particular about their digestion, or their health, or their boots, clothes, or appearance it was decidedly the reverse. However dry the soil by nature (and the Home wood was not remarkable that way), there is always a sufficient quantity of rank grass, ferns, or bog in the middle of the night under a May moon, to intimate the possibility of a cold in the head; and not unfrequently of young and vigorous thorns to make moving about in the dark exciting, to say the least of it. The fanciful and imaginative call up in such moments pictures of those they love, or of possible adders which may sting them, an allegorical parallel by no means contemplated when I began this sentence, but flowing spontaneously from the pen of one whose knowledge of the subject is happily theoretical.

Stafford Carrington and Captain Trumps were not the only persons whose sufferings might have been mitigated by tobacco, but who were restrained by a sense of duty from that indulgence; and the contrast between their present condition, and that which they had left so lately, added to their sense of 'the inconvenient.'

The trenches is dreary work; and Laurence Bradfield, by far the most philosophic of the volunteer party, could not help wondering how long they were to wait for the sport that was promised them. With his back to a tree and his legs in a tangled mass of wet grass and ferns, he may be forgiven if he doubted the pleasures of contemplation, and sighed (not aloud) for a more active exercise of his powers.

'Suppose they should not come at all,' said

Stafford Carrington to himself; 'if any intelligence has reached them that we have been put upon our guard, what fools we shall look! and how long are we to be kept in suspense?'

'I hope we shall have to fight,' said Captain Trumps, also to himself; 'I don't see the fun of sitting in this ditch till daylight and then having to walk back again.'

Lord Dallington was wondering how many months they would get when they were caught, and whether anything under six would be a sufficient recompense for an almost certain attack of gout. Lord Mentmore was fond enough of his shooting to be personally interested in the fate of his eggs; and to do Sackham justice the present gang of poachers was not that with which he had ever been in league. To say truth he had no idea of foreigners coming on his beat, and with some of them he was at deadly feud, having deserted them some five years back to get an honest livelihood, which he did in his own way. He was the only one of the party who thoroughly enjoyed these hours of inactivity; and it is astonishing how warm one is kept by a good wholesome anticipation of revenge.

It was impossible to tell exactly how long they had remained each in his uncomfortable position, which defied sleep or sentiment notwithstanding the moonlight, chequered only by fleeting clouds. It might have been one or two in the morning, when near the top of the cover a very gentle crackling of the underwood began to be heard by those nearest the base of the hill. Presently two or three hen pheasants were seen to run in the open glade, with a slight 'gluck,' not slowly, but as if alarmed, yet unwilling to quit the spot from which they had been driven. These were evident symptons that something unusual was occurring. Perhaps a cat, or a weasel, or some vermin. This was not impossible. Still the hope that it might be a termination to their suspense was cherished by the watchers about the knoll. 'Up guards and at them,' would have been a welcome sound to Laurence Bradfield or to Stafford Carrington, while Trumps and Dallington, and the rest of the watchers along either side of the broad ride, listened anxiously for a whistle in one part of the cover or the other.

At that moment, while the hens were creeping through the brushwood anxiously looking back to the nests from which they had escaped, Lord Mentmore passed close to Stafford Carrington.

'Mentmore,' said he, in a hoarse whisper. Lord Mentmore turned his head. 'Have you seen anything?'

'Yes; it's all right. Sackham's on the move; keep close till you hear the signal, and then we have then. They can't get away. Where's Bradfield?'

'Farther on, I think—but I can't see him.'

At that moment a very soft muffled sound of a small sheep-bell, scarcely distinguishable, came down the breeze.

'Ah!' said Mentmore, 'I thought so. They've the dog; it's almost light enough to have done without it, as some of them have been in the covers to-day. But it's all the better; if he moves, they must be taken. There goes one.'

A single figure, apparently armed with a thick stick, and carrying a small net, or something of the kind, passed quickly from one tree to another, whilst a shrill whistle, and the sound of a shot followed by a low moan, told that the battle had commenced in earnest. Up rose a dozen stalwart forms at once, flitting like shadows as they rushed across the bright moonlight and were again lost in the dusky shadows; all towards one point; the brow of the hill. For there stood Mr. Sackham, backed by three or four keepers, already exchanging blows with the foremost of, at least, a dozen marauders. The diversion made in his favour by the noise of the coming aid was of great and signal service. One half at least attempted to escape by the main ride; while the rest, ignorant of the numbers by whom they were beset, fought on, exchanging blows and compliments with undiminished zeal.

'Get back, Bill,' said a huge poacher, in whom the reader may recognize Mr. Dan Morton, 'get back; some of those fellows are off; it won't do to stop here,' and acting on the advice he retreated before Sackham, who was vigorously defending one of his men already down. A few seconds, however, brought up the reserves, and in an instant Stapleton, Wilfred Jones, and Stafford Carrington were struggling with their assailants. Lord Mentmore went straight to the poor fellow on the ground, clearing his way with a vigorous blow from a short cudgel, which he carried, and which took effect on the wrist of a scoundrel about to disable Sackham at the very moment.

'What is it, Sackham, badly wounded—gunshot?'

'No, no, my lord, that was only the dog; blow on the head—get him some water; I must have the big stranger,' and the keeper pressed forward after Dan Morton. At that moment, however, there appeared on the scene a new character, Mr. Job Fletcher.

Job Fletcher had his notions of honour and chivalry; and though he was not particular now about taking a few pheasants that did not belong to him, he thought the desertion of a brother vagabond in difficulties a grievous sin. Upon my honour I think Job Fletcher had high notions of what is gentlemanly, which never have squared with the strictest rules of *meum* and *tuum*. Well! Job, accustomed to poaching in a quiet way, where the keepers knew him and where the bench of magistrates knew him, was a little out of his element in this heavy affair. At the first sound of a mighty army of assailants he had acted upon impulse, and turned to make the best of his own way back, with his companions. No sooner, however, had he had time for reflection than it occurred to him that Dan, who was a stranger like himself, might want his assistance. At all events they ought both to row in the same boat. So Job the dishonest very honourably made his way back to the scene of conflict he had quitted. There is honour, though not honesty, among thieves.

Job Fletcher, we have said, was a fine, handsome young fellow, just the shape and make for a prize-fighter, worth two of Dan Morton, and not deficient in natural science, which is an anomalous expression, but comprehensible to most of my readers. He straightway engaged Mr. Sackham, by a tremendous left-hander, which staggered that worthy official, and which would have been repeated with effect but for the intervention of Lord Mentmore and Wilfred Jones, who, having ascertained that his servant was not shot, but merely disabled by a blow, left him to somebody else, and went to the assistance of the keeper.

'Never mind about me,' said Job, addressing Dan Morton. 'You be off, you fool; it's only a three months' job.' He continued to fight vigorously, as if he preferred to avoid even that contingency. 'Be off, Dan, and tell the old woman it's all right.'

Dan balanced in his mind whether this sensible advice was to be taken, and having upon his mind something a little heavier than the 'poaching of eggs,' had just determined upon saving himself, as the aspect of affairs showed him he could not do much to save his friend. The best intentions, however, lose their value by being formed too late. On the collar of Dan's coat a hand was at that moment placed, which, having just disposed of a poacher, may be said to have warmed to its work. The other hand held menacingly a short stick, which, as he turned round to confront his foe, Dan grasped instinctively, aiming a blow at the same time, which Laurence Bradfield received upon the muscular part of the arm without much injury. The poacher did not recognize at once the young squire of Sommerton, but Bradfield knew his man to be the same whom he had seen in the gardens, believed him to be connected in some way with his own village, as the owner of the remarkable American bludgeon, and had consequently the strongest grounds for imagining that this was not their first struggle for mastery. What Dan Morton's intentions might be were not plain to Bradfield; his primary object was escape. Punishment was sure to fall heavily upon a man of his antecedents, if caught; and he had other particular reasons for not desiring six months', or even two years', hard labour at present. Bradfield, with his usual good-natured *insouciance*, but vigorous determination when roused, was bent upon disabling and capturing his father's tenant.

Blows were falling think and heavily in other parts of the wood; but the battle especially raged in the main ride and round the hill. The poachers, who had made their way down the ride towards the gate, were compelled to proceed slowly and laboriously, from the nature of the ground, followed as they were by Stapleton and others, gentlemen and keepers. As they neared the gate, a fresh band appeared in front —Trumps, Lord Dallington, and two watchers. A very short and decisive skirmish ended, in which nothing suffered but Lord Dallington's right arm, and Captain Trumps' hat. One of the poachers lay stunned and bleeding on the ground, and two more were caught and tied together by some providentially discovered cords in the pockets of Mr. Sykes.

'That's lucky,' said Sykes, deliberately uncoiling it, while four others held the unfortunate victims by the throat; 'that was meant for last week, but we wasn't so fortunate as to catch 'em.'

After this the fight seemed pretty general, and the keepers were too intent upon the care of their prisoners, and too much winded by their exertions, to do much in the way of pursuit. Mr. Sackham observed, too, 'That he knowed 'em, and knowed pretty well where to find 'em, when they was wanted.' Poor Joe was safe enough, with a companion who had stuck to him more faithfully than Dan Morton.

The latter, in the meantime, continued his struggle with Laurence Bradfield, while a little distance from them the fray had progressed amidst curses and imprecations, not always or entirely on the part of the aggressors. Blows on the head, and especially in the discharge of a duty, will make even gentlemen swear. Morton and Laurence Bradfield were pretty equally matched. An accident on either side (and they were embracing each other in a deadly struggle) might give the victory to either. At length that accident happened. As they shifted their ground, aiming ineffectual blows at each other, Morton's foot caught in a root or tangled briar; he lost his footing, and fell heavily to the ground, dragging his opponent with him, where they rolled over and over. In this case Bradfield's greater activity served him in good stead. He was quickly on his legs, and planting his knee heavily on the other's chest, he seized his wrist with one hand and his neckcloth with the other. Perceiving that Morton's stick had fallen from his grasp in the fall, he adopted this fashion of subjugation in preference to the advantage which he might have taken, and laying his weapon on one side called upon him to surrender. Morton answered sulkily, with a violent oath, and continued to struggle.

'Mentmore, Stapleford, come here, quick,' shouted Bradfield.

The former was at his side, having left his prisoners in good hands. At the same moment Sackham came up, and whipping from his pocket a light dog chain, the three were not long in securing the arms of the powerful ruffian, so as effectually to quiet him. The battle was over; and though the account is long to relate, it had not lasted ten minutes from the time of its commencement to the capture of the prisoners. Six of them were helplessly captive.

The first thing to be done was to place them in the middle of their captors, and march them to the house; and as the moon was now up, and all need for concealment over, it was not difficult to manage. The owner and his guests, the keepers and their assistants, formed a strong body-guard which it would have been impossible to break through. Before starting, however, it was necessary to take stock of the victors, who had not achieved success without some losses.

'Trumps, your hat seems to have suffered.'

'It has; and has not quite saved my head,' said he, applying his hand to a very prominent bruise, which had been partially averted. The thickness of even a guardsman's skull would not have withstood the assault, but for his hat.

'And your coat,' added another, observing that garment to be in a somewhat tattered condition.

'That's not mine; my head and my hat are. Mentmore's valet insisted upon lending me his master's coat, as we came away.'

On looking round, there was a manifest deficiency of neckcloths, and a pocket-handkerchief or two were declared to be missing. Stafford Carrington had lost a valuable cigar case, having been down in the *mêlée.* Of wounds, Lord Dallington's was the most severe, one arm being quite disabled. Lord Mentmore himself had a blow on the cheek, which was flushed and swollen; while the most discomposed in toilette, but the least apparently hurt, and the most composed in mind, was Laurence Bradfield. One or two of the keepers had had some sharp fighting, and exhibited signs of it externally.

'Now,' said Mentmore, 'are you ready, Sackham? Let's be off. Oh! untie those poor devils' arms; they can't get away now, if you put them into the middle.'

'Don't trust 'em, my lord; I knows 'em.'

'Then loosen the cord, and strap each of them by the wrist to a sound keeper; they can't move as they're tied now.'

Mr. Sackham, with assistance, did as he was bid.

'To-morrow morning you had better come and pick up the lost property. Now then, march.' And they did march, to Silvermere.

'And now, my lord, what's to be done with 'em? it's only two o'clock.'

'You must untie them, and lock them safely into some place until the morning. Send a man over to Coppernails for a proper escort, and we'll have them taken there to-morrow. Get warrants made out, and have them before the magistrates on Saturday.'

All which things were done, with one only exception; which defect under the circumstances could not well be helped. They appeared before the magistrates, save only the greatest ruffian of them all—Mr. Daniel Morton. His absence can be accounted for.

When Lord Mentmore and his guests had dressed their wounds, and they and their sleepy valets had retired to bed, Mr. Sackham selected fit and proper places, as he thought, for his prisoners. Two were placed in one room, with a watch outside; three were placed in another equally secure; and Dan Morton was shut up in a small untenanted room adjoining the rest, which was accommodated with iron bars to the windows, and a strong lock and chain to the door. A sentinel was added, with injunctions to pay frequent visits to see that his prisoner was right; and then Mr. Sackham betook himself to the back-kitchen, a fire, a pipe, and a pewter, and fell asleep.

Nor is it much to be wondered at, that, after having once looked in upon Dan, and finding him with his eyes hermetically sealed, his sentinel should have done the same as Mr. Sackham.

excepting the pipe, pot, and the kitchen-fire. He only fell asleep, under greater difficulties.

Dan Morton was, in the matter of sleep, a perfect weasel. So he began to think as soon as he was alone, and his thoughts took a natural turn—how to get out of the scrape at the smallest expense.

I have said that he had long been hampered by his doubts as to turning the documents he had stolen from Sommerton into a profitable investment. Circumstances now suggested Mr. Laurence Bradfield as the fittest recipient of those papers. The reasons were obvious. They concerned him nearly; he would give as much money, or as many promises, as his father; he was near at hand; and he would add to it all the active influence (as Dan foolishly thought) he could to get his present punishment as favourably considered as possible. A *suppressio veri* seems to a poor man a venial fault, and a *corruption of justice* an easy expedient, where money or position are brought to bear.

One other sentiment remained over and above, which is scarcely worth mentioning, but that he had few virtues to throw away—he felt some gratitude and a fair share of admiration for the way in which Laurence Bradfield had fought the battle. Having made up his mind to the course he should pursue, he bethought him of the papers which he still carried about with him. He dived at once into his pocket to take a last look at them, and to assure himself of their reality: for they were very like a bank post-bill, which one likes to pass in review occasionally, lest it shall have escaped altogether. As he put his hands, first into one pocket, then into another, a spectator would have been struck with the change of countenance in Dan Morton. First it was red, a roseate hue suffused his face, and drops of perspiration stood upon his brow. This lasted for a few seconds while he searched sedulously the pockets of his shooting-jacket, in which he had usually carried it. Then he transferred his attention to a side-pocket, in which he felt a conviction that it *was not*. By slow degrees the perspiration became cold, and then he knew that his features became deadly pale—that a sickly hue overspread them; and he clenched his knotted hands as he summoned up the occurrences of the last few hours. Where had he left it? in that cursed wood? He had dropped it.

In searching his pockets for the missing deed, he had found something which might be of service. It set him thinking again. At this moment his gaoler moved outside. It was then that he was overtaken by sudden and heavy sleep. No sooner, however, had his gaoler retired, than he rose slowly and stealthily, and examined the window and its bars. He took from his pocket his newly-discovered assistant. He removed from around the bars the tightly-fitting mortar. In twenty minutes it was loosened; in half-an-hour the bar shook to his well-applied and gigantic strength. In a few more minutes it was out; and in another five Dan Morton was out too.

His first move was to the wood. Alas! the moon had hidden her light; clouds obscured her face; and his search was unsuccessful. He dared not stay to meet the dawn; for he knew that before long his flight would be discovered, and wreckers would be rife around the hill—the scene of battle. And so it was that before dawn Dan Morton was miles away.

The fate of the rest is obvious. The stolidity of one gentleman, who had made his money in trade, and who had no interest in game, but whose hen-roosts were defended by law, was not sufficient in this instance to refute the testimony of so many to an aggravated assault, and the poachers were committed to take their trial; when, in due course of time, they received, each according to his merits, the reward of his deeds.

As Bradfield sat alone in Lord Mentmore's library on the following morning, wondering how long the present Ministry would last with its foreign policy, Lord Mentmore's servant entered.

'Mr. Sackham has been to the wood, sir, and brought back a quantity of sticks and neckerchiefs. He found Mr. Carrington's cigar-case, sir; and he thinks this must belong to you.' At the same time Mr. Stubbs put into the hands of Bradfield a paper, torn and soiled, whose writing was yellow, and whose edges were black, bearing on the outside the word 'Sommerton.'

Bradfield thanked the valet, opened it, glanced hastily at the contents, nodded his head, and Mr. Stubbs quitted the room.

CHAPTER VIII.

LAURENCE BRADFIELD BEGINS TO ACT.

'What thine heart findeth to do, do it with all thy might.'

THREE or four days after the affray with the poachers, the week's sport ended with some private racing in the park, and the party broke up. Evelyn Carrington and Ellen Bradfield had improved the opportunity which this visit had given them to become more intimately acquainted. Mrs. Bradfield felt flattered and happy at an evident predilection for her daughter; and Lady Carrington was not able to resist the natural beauty and sense which her daughter's friend displayed. There was a little similarity between the characters of the two; and although Ellen had not pride of birth, which was natural to Lady Carrington, and which had even been increased by her marriage, she had a more genuine pride of her own.

If Lady Carrington had suspected the true state of the case, or of the feeling which was growing rapidly in her son towards Ellen Bradfield, she would probably, but vainly, have striven to withdraw; but Carrington was a very undemonstrative person—he was apparently indifferent and unimpulsive—not likely to fall in love, so people thought, without a very sufficient cause; and very susceptible withal of a certain ridicule, which he, commonly with others, attached to victims of the tender passion.

Stafford Carrington had been, in the first place, like his friend Lord Mentmore, attracted by the personal beauty of Ellen Bradfield. It had occurred to him quite suddenly, and in spite of a powerful but irrational prejudice against the name. There was no such thing in either the one or the other of these men as love at first sight. Mentmore was too cautious; and Carrington, by habit of mind, incapable of such a thing. But the beauty of the girl was so radiant, so commanding, yet of so delicate a character; the mixture of the conqueror and of the captive was so subtilely blended in her beautiful liquid eyes, whose usual expression was one of partial surprise, in her straightly-cut features, her short curled vermilion lip, the decision of a marked under jaw, and the luxuriant richness of her wavy golden hair, that few men resisted the influence of her charms. Had she been like some women she would have lived in a halo of unpremeditated conquest. Her decision of manner, and total absence of coquetry, preserved her victims from self-immolation and herself from the slightest taint of calumny. In the society in which she moved (and great wealth commands a position in this country), it was felt that the manufacturer's daughter might worthily aspire to the highest honours.

Mentmore thought so too. Since his former visit to the house, he had been accustoming himself to regard Miss Bradfield as essential to his happiness, capable of adorning his home, and of putting an end to those preposterous pretensions to the management of Silvermere by certain dowager ladies and their aspiring daughters, which Mentmore was too clever not to see, and too generous ruthlessly to trample upon. Lady Elizabeth, his aunt, had long counselled such a step; and had she known the state of his finances, and the inroad Newmarket and Leicestershire had made upon his princely fortune, she would have thought it none the worst that the lady should have been able to pay handsomely for the honour. I need scarcely say that this was not an item which entered into Mentmore's calculations.

During the visit to Silvermere his attentions had been at the service equally of all his guests. When he could do so without infringement of etiquette, he had endeavoured to distinguish Ellen Bradfield by some little mark of kindness, by word, by look, or by actual courtesy, which could not, as he imagined, have failed to strike her. Indeed they did so; and she had never failed to exhibit the gratification she felt. Externally Lord Mentmore and Miss Bradfield were fast friends, mutually pleased with each other, and wanting but time and sunshine to ripen the fruit of such an intimacy. How very little we know of one another; and how unjust we are to women!

The fact is that this easy acceptance of little favours, delicate attentions, and the ready expression of thanks for them is not a sign of love; it may be that the seed is sown, but these are no signs of its having taken root. Yet these are the women that some men call coquettes, when a too facile interpretation of their kindness induces a premature proposal, which is refused. Mentmore had seen hundreds of women jump at the same sort of attentions, and knew that they only waited for the favourable moment. Women hate to give pain, as a rule. But they are not all equally expansive in their desires or their demonstrations.

When Bradfield had retired to his room,

which he did after pretending to finish the newspaper he was reading, he drew slowly from his pocket the paper which had been placed in his hands by Mr. Stubbs. He was anxious to ascertain how far that gentleman or any of his friends had profited by the opportunity given them of ascertaining the contents of the document. He rang his bell, and desired his servant to ask Mr. Stubbs to come to him for a moment.

'Will you tell me, Mr. Stubbs, who brought this paper from the wood?'

'Yes, sir—it was one of the watchers; he said he found it on the hill, at least at the foot of it, and as he couldn't read, sir, he asked me what it was. I opened it, sir, and I saw it was some old paper about a release of the Somerton property; and as I saw your name, I thought of course it was yours.' The answer plainly showed that the man was speaking the truth.

'Thank you, Stubbs, it belongs to my father. Mr. Stubbs backed himself out.

Three or four days after the party broke up. The Carringtons and the Bradfields travelled together, with the exception of Laurence Bradfield, who had gone to London the day before. On his arrival he found the season commencing in earnest. It was seven in the evening, and carriages were hastening through the streets to their several engagements. It was a bright warm evening immediately after the recess, and he was greeted by several of his parliamentary friends as he turned down St. James's Street. Those who spoke to him failed to notice any change. He was, however, listless, *distrait;* his mind was full of incertitude and vague anxiety. But men are very slow in their perceptions of this kind, and, full of their own schemes and interests, regard but slightly those of other people. A woman would have seen it in a minute; but Laurence Bradfield eschewed the drawing-rooms of his acquaintance, and went straight to his club.

He read his letters. His father was in Sommerton still—very busy, and venting his ill-humour in the county, which had quietly submitted to the imposition of Stafford Carrington, and seemed very well satisfied with its burthen. Then he dined, and although exceedingly anxious to have a little privacy, and time for thought and determination, he found himself unable to get it among questions on the coming debate, the Two Thousand, Lord Crossover's stud, New Tenor, the Law of Marriage in Scotland, and the Retirement of the late Master of the Pytchley. At length the day was done; artificial light had assumed the place of the waning sun in the streets; and lighting a cigar, and putting on a warm overcoat, he strolled into Pall Mall.

Within ten minutes his mind was made up upon the first steps to be taken.

John Grosse Codicil was a man of the highest reputation as a solicitor; he occupied a high position, which he had attained by hard work, brains, and money-lending, when it was a profitable business among the fast men of a previous generation. When Crockford required ready-money, Codicil had to find it.

He had long retired into a magnificent house, and indisputable respectability; but he still was accessible to men of position, and kept his name up on the firm, though younger men did the business.

John Grosse Codicil had shared the confidence of the first Mr. Bradfield, and the present proprietor of Sommerton, with the Darvilles. The latter solicitors being purely of provincial fame, had nothing to do with the northern estates and money matters of the ironmaster. Their business was almost wholly confined to his Midland property. In person, the old man was tall, thin, grey-haired, not bald, almost unbent. He was a scrupulous dresser, had the appearance and manners of a gentleman, and retained only a few provincialisms, which had clung to him tenaciously from his earliest youth. At half-past nine in the evening in question, he was drinking his glass of rare port, while the lady whom he designated his housekeeper was preparing his coffee in another room. He sat without closing his curtains, and his silk handkerchief was spread over his head ready for repose, when he was roused by a knock at the door.

Mr. Laurence Bradfield's card and candles were brought in at the same time.

'Is Mrs. Tanner in the next room?'

'Yes, sir.'

'Then ask Mr. Bradfield to walk in here.'

The servant retired, and returned ushering in Laurence Bradfield.

After an apology for the lateness of his visit, and a disclaimer from the old lawyer, Laurence continued,

'What I particularly wish to know is, whether you can give me any information about the Sommerton property.'

'That is exactly the subject on which I should have consulted you,' replied Mr. Codicil, shading his eyes from the light, and speculating upon the probability of his old client's son wanting a loan.

'I mean on its purchase, title, and mortgages

upon it, if any exist. You forget I was not born at the time, and have scarcely lived there since half-a-dozen years altogether.'

'Your grandfather bought it, Mr. Bradfield, for little money. In other words, he bought the interest of other parties in it, to whom it was mortgaged, but redeemable within a certain number of years. The property was not redeemed within the specified time, and it lapsed into your grandfather's hands. The title, I believe, is excellent; and it must be worth, with its iron works, at least four times the purchase-money. Yet—stay—one moment, Mr. Laurence; there might be a difficulty. I cannot refer here; but I think there was some understanding that it was to be settled on the females, with only a reversion to yourself. You have a sister, I believe?'

'Yes, I have; though that scarcely enters into the question.'

'Excuse me, it's the main point. Money might be raised by thousands by other means. In your case, personal security—'

'My dear sir,' said Laurence, rather amused in the midst of his anxiety, 'I don't want money.'

The old gentleman took down his hand from his eyes, as if such a phenomenon were not commonly to be seen there.

'Oh!—ah!—I see—that's another matter: then I'm sorry I have delayed you. The fact is, the Darvilles of Saxonby had the business. They bought the property, or rather the interests of the original mortgagee, and I am sure he would give you every information. I have but a very limited acquaintance with the purchase.'

'And our title?'

'Is as good as any in the world. That's certain; because some quarrel gave rise to a trial, a most ill-judged proceeding, some five-and-thirty years ago, upon the presumption that the money had been paid and the property redeemed within the time. Sir Reginald Carrington borrowed a quantity of money from me to pay his personal debts: he was the most accomplished man alive, and the most needy. Not a particle of evidence was adduced that the money had been paid; and certainly no receipt or acknowledgment could be found, or had ever been heard of. Anything I can do for you, Mr. Bradfield, I shall be delighted; but Hugh Darville has always done the business at Sommerton, and done it well, I believe.'

Bradfield thanked the lawyer, and walked home. His anxieties were not by any means at an end, not even allayed by his visit. The paper, however, might be a forgery for some malicious purpose, and the sooner the mystery was cleared up the better. So the next day towards evening, having attended the business of the House in the morning, he took the train for Saxonby.

It was late when he reached Saxonby; so he ordered a fly from the station to take him to Sommerton. In passing through the town, however, on his road, he caught sight of a light in Scarsdale's window. It was not a blaze of light, such as that with which a bachelor curate is wont to greet his friends when he assembles them round a hospitable board; it was rather the feeble glimmer of one seeking that quiet, or guarding that retirement, which was now to be broken in upon. On a given signal the flyman stopped, and the neat, good-looking little maid—smiles, ribbons, and braid—came to the door.

'Is Mr. Scarsdale alone?'

'Yes, sir,' said she; 'you can walk up. Stay, sir; there's no light.'

'Coachman, I shall not want you, I think, to go to Sommerton to-night. Order me a bed at the "Bear."'

He ascended the stairs, and Scarsdale's maid-of-all-work knocked at the door, and opened it at the same moment. It was a very feeble apology, that knock, for the boldness of intrusion.

Scarsdale was 'done up' for the night, as he thought. The kettle boiled away on the hob; on the table were glasses and a spirit-decanter;

the master himself was dressed in a light smoking-jacket, almost recumbent in an arm-chair. He was reading a good book, and smoking a pretty good cigar.

'Nothing the matter, I hope, Bradfield?' said he; his thoughts recurring at once to his parish, and fearing something might be wrong at the Hall.

'Nothing whatever, my good friend; and therefore, if you will give me a glass of hot gin-and-water, I'll sit down and smoke a cigar with you. I want to talk to you about myself.' And lighting a cigar, and taking the opposite side of the fireplace, he began to smoke too.

If gin-and-water and cigars are favourable to conversation, they are no less so to concealment of purpose and feeling. Had they not been so, it is possible that his friend might have detected a difference from his usual quiet, idle manner to that which now characterized his movements. His voice, too, was eager, which was quite unnatural to him; and he changed his seat once or twice while speaking, eventually standing with his back to the fire.

After a little time, and when a pause in the conversation came, which it is sure to do when one or both of the speakers are thinking upon different or irrelevant subjects, he said abruptly, turning his cigar round, and pretending to look at it very critically,

'Scarsdale, I want to speak to you.'

'Then I think I can guess what it is.'

'I think not;' and Laurence Bradfield again twisted his cigar with great care.

'Marriage, Laurence? I congratulate you.'

'Why should that be the subject on which I wish to consult you?'

'The old and the sick and the poor consult me on other points, but not the young and the strong and the wealthy.'

'At all events, you're wrong this time. Listen, Scarsdale, there may be nothing in what I have to say, it may involve much. Since I have been down at Lord Mentmore's something has happened;' the glow deepened on Scarsdale's face, but the candlelight did not betray him.

'Miss Bradfield,' said he, with the fortitude of a martyr. 'I'm glad to hear it; a most brilliant prospect, and one of the best fellows in the world.'

'Wrong again; don't guess any more. The racing prophets are better than you, and they are exceedingly bad.' Laurence Bradfield then told Scarsdale of the poaching expedition, of his meeting with Dan Morton and Job Fletcher, and eventually of the paper which had been brought to him on the following morning. 'That document contains a very extraordinary announcement.'

'And where did it come from?'

'Doubtless from the pocket of one of those marauders.'

'Did you not ascertain?'

'No; the one I suspect made his escape, and though there is a warrant out against him, he has not yet been traced;' he drew from his pocket as he spoke the paper in question; 'there, read that.'

As Scarsdale rather spelt than read the paper of which mention has so frequently been made, his astonishment gradually subsided into one long-drawn sigh. It contained a simple release of the Sommerton property by Mr. Henry Bradfield to Sir Reginald Carrington. It bore date May 29th, 1820. Enclosed in the same paper was, at the same time, a receipt signed by the same person for a sum of three thousand five hundred pounds, being the last instalment due on the Sommerton property. Scarsdale sat for a minute or two, spell-bound.

'Now, Scarsdale, what do you think of that? and how came it in the hands of Mr. Dan Morton?'

'What do I think of it? Laurence, are you sure, do you know that this is your grandfather's signature?'

Bradfield brightened a little at the possibility of escaping from a conviction. He took the paper and looked again closely at it; and then said in a low, husky voice, 'Indeed, I believe it is; it exactly resembles those I have seen, and is very peculiar.'

'That peculiarity might have made it less difficult to imitate.'

'No; I think it is his; the paper, the writing, is manifestly of the date assigned to it. Scarsdale, you know something of this;' this was said with an energy, that carried conviction. Scarsdale was not proof against the impulse.

'I know nothing of this; but I have some knowledge of the circumstances connected with this business. What does this involve? Your loss of property?'

'Not mine, Scarsdale; the Sommerton property belongs to my sister.' Scarsdale uttered a half-suppressed groan. 'Yes, it's hard upon her, poor girl; but she need never know poverty; and if she should, I never knew anyone who would better grace it.'

'You speak coldly of its disadvantages.'

'They are always magnified; but there's

more than this. I fear for my father. You don't know his temper, his susceptibility, and uncontrolled feelings; his impatience of disappointment; and Scarsdale, Scarsdale, if there should be disgrace, dishonour fall upon him, upon the house he has striven to found, at the sacrifice of everything really valuable—'

'You conjure up more serious ills than exist. I have heard something of this before, and it is—yes! I know you, Bradfield, and it is better that you should know all;' and Scarsdale rose from his seat and went to his desk. He brought out the torn and soiled note which he had received from Giles Morton in the workhouse, and placed it in the hands of his friend. 'There, Laurence, when we know the worst we can take the better steps to remedy the evil.' Laurence read,

'"*May* 13, 1820.

'"If Sir Reginald Carrington will do me the honour of coming to Patcham on Wednesday, the 29th inst., I shall be happy to give the release, which is already prepared, on the receipt of Sir Reginald's cheque, or note of hand for the balance of the mortgage.

'"I have the honour to be, Sir,

'"Your obedient servant,

'"HENRY BRADFIELD.

'"To Sir Reginald Carrington, Bart."'

With trembling hand, but steady and determined will, the young man compared the dates, the writing, and the very paper mark. They were the same; and as he sat down, faint from their perusal, he folded his arms, and looked quietly up in his friend's face for further intelligence. He was unable to speak.

Scarsdale then proceeded to give a detailed account of his conversations with old Morton in the Saxonby Union. He held out some hopes which he himself had derived from the the state of the man's mind, and from the remarks of Hugh Darville. He pointed to the probability of some rascality which was not yet fathomed; of the probable innocence of his grandfather; of the money never having been paid him, although the release had been prepared; of the likelihood of the money and the release having been stolen, and neither having reached their destination; he urged the arguments which Hugh Darville had made use of, and which he himself had set at nought.

Bradfield was quieted, but not convinced. He had so much at stake that he dreaded the consequences. His mother, his sister, above all, his father; for he felt that he had sometimes judged him harshly, and added to his irritation; and generous minds forget their provocations when the authors of them are in trouble. He thought but little of himself; but he had his own burthen to bear. How should he again present himself before Evelyn Carrington, when his father's long usurpation should be revealed? He was saved the bitter pain of knowing that his very name was distasteful to Sir Michael, and that long prejudice would be gratefully revived by such a catastrophe as the present.

'You should have mentioned these things, Scarsdale,' said he, with some impatience, 'to my father at the time; better that we should have sought out means to do justice and right before it was forced upon us by accident.'

Scarsdale was obliged to tell him of their quarrel, and of the effect it had in estranging him from the house; but he did not tell him that there was another cause which held his hand from the infliction of pain.

They separated late; but it was settled before they parted, that the next day Hugh Darville should be taken into his counsel, and that time and consideration should be called to his aid before any publicity need be given to the affair.

'The sins of the fathers,' said Scarsdale, to himself, 'are visited upon the children even in this world; but it is difficult to attach serious discredit to them for anything which happened before they were born.'

CHAPTER IX.

HE TAKES COUNSEL, BUT NOT COMFORT.

'Vos lene consilium et datis, et dato
Gaudetis almæ.'—HOR. : *Odes*, lib. iii. 4.

THE difference of temperament in these two men, equally honourable and in some things equally prudent, would have been shown in the manner either would have acted under the same circumstances. Had Scarsdale been in Bradfield's situation he would not have slept before he had proceeded to unravel the mystery which surrounded him. He would, possibly that very night, have knocked up Darville to see how far he could assist him; he would certainly have visited the lawyer upon an empty stomach the next morning. He would have issued emissaries in search of Mr. Dan Morton, and he would have rushed straight off, documents in hand, to Sir Michael Carrington, and have run the risk of a great amount of needless and irreparable mischief. Laurence Bradfield slept well and soundly, although he felt sufficiently the possible difficulties of his case. When he woke he revised it carefully. It was the loss to his sister of a magnificent estate; to himself it raised up inconveniences and distresses, which as they affected him more slowly than other men were likely to affect him more deeply. He felt that; but it never quickened his pulse. He was determined to do justice, cost him what it might, but he meant to do it with such deliberation as should leave no room for regret, no need for retrogression. Altogether, with his own feelings, his sister's position, his mother's gentle patience, who, he knew, would feel most and say the least about it, and above all his father's critical position, which could, however, be cleared by a single word, as he hoped, he had plenty to think of, and therefore was in less haste to act.

It was midday before he called upon Darville.

The people in Saxonby saluted him as he walked down the street; and many thought they had never seen a finer-looking fellow, as with a slow deliberate walk he almost lounged along, a head taller, and many inches broader than most whom he met. He looked in their faces too, with his bright blue eyes, as honestly and openly as the god of day himself, and Mr. Brand and Mr. Parrott made some comparisons between fathers and sons, not complimentary to the former.

Before we get into Hugh Darville's private room, the reader may as well enter a more private sanctum, Hugh Darville's conscience.

Hugh Darville was not a bad man; he was kind and generous, warm-tempered and enthusiastic; not of high principles, nor a high sense of honour; but there are thousands worse, as there are thousands better. His was a mixed character, with perhaps the good predominating.

The way in which he became involved in Mr. Bradfield's affairs at all was purely accidental, and requires us to go back to a distant date, when the present generation was young. He became possessed in early life of a knowledge which was dangerous, by one of those circumstances, which happen to his profession, in which men with more firmness and principle, or as some will have it with less temptation, act differently.

Henry Bradfield died; somewhat suddenly, certainly inopportunely. He left his affairs, prosperous in the highest degree, in some confusion, arising from a bad habit of trusting nobody. His son, sent for at the last moment, and not knowing much of the new property which had come into the family, as he presumed by legitimate purchase, placed the business in the hands of Mr. Darville, senior, the most respectable solicitor for many miles round. It so happened that a severe attack of illness prevented the old gentleman from paying that personal attention to it, which a client of such importance, pecuniarily speaking, invariably enjoys at his solicitor's hands. Young Darville, an extravagant young man, fresh from

London, Cambridge, and a Continental tour, and not long married, was destined to supply the place of his father, at a critical moment, and within a very short period of that father's death.

Amongst the papers, documentary and testamentary, which fell into his hands was one, manifestly not intended for him; one which contained a secret, almost a confession, involving the reputation of Abel Bradfield, and the possession of the Sommerton property. It was evident that oversight had left it among those papers, which are generally placed in the hands of the family solicitor, as matters of business. It should have been seen by no one but by Abel Bradfield, for whom it was intended, and to whom it was addressed. The purport of it is soon stated. It admitted, in simple terms, the existence of a release and receipt for the mortgage money for the Sommerton Estate; it owned without much remorse and with some exultation the deception and robbery that had been practised upon the Carrington family, as a set-off against the proud and insolent spirit with which the mortgagee had been treated in all transactions by the mortgagor. It forgot, or intentionally omitted to say, where this extraordinary document was to be found; and it rather implied that the testator would not die less happily, if the heir to the Sommerton property proved as callous and indifferent to the claims of justice as he, Henry Bradfield, himself had done. Whether this was intended as a draft of what would be a letter to Abel Bradfield to be opened after his father's death, or whether it was positively lost and not recovered, amidst the numberless papers belonging to a man of no education, no business habits, and with a multiplicity of irons in the fire, is impossible to say. There the letter was, when Hugh Darville was ordered, in a spirit of assumed importance, to run his eye over 'those stupid papers;' when Mr. Abel Bradfield felt the consequence which newly-acquired wealth gives to a vain person of five-and-twenty.

He did run his eye over the papers, and,

understanding the value of this one, put it in his pocket.

Circumstances, more than anything else, determined him as to its destination. Within three days he was sent for on business by Mr. Abel Bradfield. That business was to read, in the presence of the old man, and witness the signature of, his will. Mr. Henry Bradfield, although at his last gasp, was perfectly sensible. He had, however, been attacked by paralysis, which rendered his speech very imperfect. There was nothing in his state, however, to call for immediate apprehension, when Hugh Darville left the room, having accomplished all that was required of him.

Five minutes more and a bell rung violently. It was followed by the hasty footsteps of a valet, old Mr. Bradfield's favourite servant. Mr. Abel was wanted immediately, and he went. The old man was dying. He held with one hand metaphorically to life, with the other, physically to his son. A great struggle was apparent. The eyes dilated—the lips formed inarticulate words. He called plainly on the names of Carrington and Giles Morton. He spoke of the room below that in which he was dying, pointing energetically towards it, and uttering the word—'release, release,' several times in succession. His valet was sent over for Probewell, and the dying man was left with his son alone. Abel Bradfield strained every nerve to catch his meaning. Suddenly the old man seemed to recover a little, and with a vast effort, he said,—

'God forgive me—the wrong I have done—not yours—not yours, my boy. Give it back—all—all—the release—the release.'

His head fell back upon his pillow, and Henry Bradfield was no more.

The disclosures which took place between these two men, led almost necessarily to the inference that there existed somewhere a release of the bond or mortgage on the Sommerton property; that that estate belonged once more wholly and solely to the Carrington family; that Giles Morton was somehow the agent employed by old Henry Bradfield in his treachery; but that the necessary documents to prove all this were in the power of Abel Bradfield, involuntarily, at least, as far as concerned their concealment. And why did these two men confide in one another? Abel Bradfield was surprised into trusting Hugh Darville, for he had no one else in whom to confide. Darville had a better motive for resigning his discovery into the hands of the man to whom it belonged, and leaving him to act upon it as he thought fit. Had Darville been a man of honour and of courage, he would at once have urged the necessity of making a proper disclosure to Sir Michael Carrington, or have threatened to have done so himself. It was the duty of both to have made every exertion, and taken every step, to have ascertained their true position. Neither had courage or honesty for this trial; and the temptation was too much for them. Bradfield had a direct object—the accumulation of wealth, the fulfiment of his ambition; and at that moment he was deep in speculations in the

North, which required increased wealth for their development. What he might have done, had he then been in the enjoyment of his present affluence, nobody can say. Darville was overcome by a sudden temptation to err in the prospect of immunity and professional success. Once having been guilty of this concealment, his life had been one of regret, but not of repentance. He never dared retrace his false steps; and at the present moment could better bear the stings of his own conscience than the taunts of a society he had outraged. One other circumstance confirmed their resolutions. Every agent or supposed witness (for they knew but of one—Giles Morton) was away from the country. Would Abel Bradfield desire to find the missing papers? Certainly not, at first. Their absence was an easy solution of his difficulty. Later, when urged to it by Hugh Darville, he would have found them; but he had then assumed sufficient courage to have destroyed them.

Since Darville's conversation with Scarsdale,

he had felt the probability of a discovery. The confession of Giles Morton, the evident complicity of his son in the plot, and the whole circumstances of the case, tended to produce that impression. From the moment he conceived this probability, he made up his mind to do what many such men would have done—to do anything he could to further the ends of justice without implicating his patron, if possible—at all hazards without criminating himself. That is a principle of English law, which he chose to consider it criminal to transgress. But he had other reasons for endeavouring to shield his client. It is true that he had occasionally suffered from his irritability and insolence; and at times he had been goaded almost into a desire for revenge, even at the sacrifice of his own reputation. But these feelings were as transient as any others to unstable minds. They were peculiarly so in his case, for he had a sincere respect for Laurence Bradfield, and almost an affection for his sister. Her little intercourse with this unprincipled lawyer had enslaved him, much as she had enslaved her other admirers. With the children of Sir Michael he had enjoyed a more restricted intimacy; they were greater people. With Abel Bradfield's family he was more at home, and circumstances had made their acquaintance more close. He had known them better, and loved them more. Besides this, he had determined to be guided by circumstances as they arose; all weak men are. The strong guide the circumstances.

'Well! Darville, how are you?' said Laurence, entering the room, and addressing him as if he saw him every day of the week instead of about three times a-year.

'Bless me! Laurence, how you startled me. It seems an age since I saw you.'

'I want your advice, if you can give it me.'

'With pleasure; sit down. Now, what is it?'

'Something about Sommerton; and, I suppose, I can apply to you with a certainty of your knowing all about it.'

'Well, I ought to know something about it. My father bought, and I have received the rents of it. It is a fine property, perhaps, the finest property of its size in the county.'

'Can it be money?' thought Darville, 'or can it be this terrible business?' He was soon undeceived.

'I had a long conversation with Scarsdale last night; and some information he gave me, and some I received elsewhere, have caused me anxiety.'

'I can hardly imagine anxiety and Laurence Bradfield coupled.' And, perhaps, at that moment there was as much anxiety in Hugh Darville as in the other.

'Then, read that.' And without more ado he placed in the lawyer's hand the paper which had been found in the wood at Silvermere.

Darville's face underwent a change, notwithstanding his preparation for what was coming; for the last person whom he expected to find the possessor of the release sat before him. Thousands of emotions passed in a minute through his mind; and conclusions the most contradictory chased each other through his brain as rapidly as the cold drops of perspiration rose upon his forehead. The nature of Laurence Bradfield, however, was not a suspicious one, and he attributed to another cause the emotions which seemed for some moments to overpower his adviser. At last Hugh Darville spoke.

'And how did you become possessed of this document? Excuse this question, but to act efficiently, we must act in concert.'

Bradfield gave him a full account of his meeting with Dan Morton, and his suspicions of that person.

'Of course, you have no idea how he became possessed of it?'

'Indeed, I have. I think he stole it from my father's house on the night of the Saxonby ball.'

Darville pondered again. Laurence Bradfield seemed to know too much, or to conjecture too accurately.

'And, why?'

Lawrence related his previous encounter with the poacher, and the capture of his stick.

'That stick,' added, he 'was a remarkable one, and has been identified as his by Nanny Fletcher.'

They sat silently looking at one another. The evidence had brought them to Sommerton.

'And where is Dan Morton?'

'God knows,' said the young man, 'I wish I did. Had Job Fletcher anything to do with this business?'

'None, none,' said Darville, in a confident tone. 'He was a child, nay, I should think, not born.'

'Has this Dan Morton any friends of his youth with whom he associates? Think. You know the neighbourhood.'

He did think, and replied, 'None.'

'None at Newmarket?' demanded Bradfield.

'Newmarket,' repeated Darville. 'Ah! that's possible. There is some man there, a trainer; I've heard something of this before. Dan Morton has many trades you know. Prize-fighter, poacher, housebreaker, tout. Yes, there is some man—'

'Then we must find him out, Darville. Such men never act alone in such matters. In a multitude of counsellors there is danger as well as wisdom. One word more. My poor father, was he—have you—that is, any suspicion that he can have known of this?'

The words came slowly, and singly out, as if every enunciation gave him pain; but he desired to know the truth, and be guided by it in his measures.

'Your father, Laurence, oh! impossible—that is—certainly not.'

The young man was only half convinced. In any other he would have repelled the suspicion as an insult: he could not do so in himself.

Before two days were over, Hugh Darville, on his own account, had made himself master of all the antecedents of Mr. Jackson from his earliest years to his trainership under Lord Mentmore. There were some curious revelations among them, and Dan Morton had played his part in them.

CHAPTER X.

UN EMBARRAS DE RICHESSES.

'Methinks there be six Richmonds in the field.'—*Rich. III.*

In the meantime the two families had arrived safely at home. Nothing particular marked the arrival but an increased inclination to closer intimacy on the part of the elder ladies. They mutually respected, and were beginning to like, each other.

'Where are you going to-day, mamma, after lunch?' said Evelyn Carrington.

'To Mrs. Bradfield's; I'm going to call upon her. Will you go too?'

'Certainly, if you like, mamma; I was going to ride.'

'I've just ordered the carriage, Ellen; I think we ought to call and inquire for Lady

Carrington. Will you go with me?' said Mrs. Bradfield.

'I'd rather not to-day, mamma,' said Miss Bradfield. 'I should leave them to call first. I don't mean to say that they would take umbrage, but there are plenty of good-natured people who would say we wanted their acquaintance.'

'My dear, that's absurd,' said simple-minded Mrs. Bradfield; 'after all the kind things they said and did at Silvermere; besides, they asked us to go over as early as possible.'

'I think Ellen is right, my dear mother; I wouldn't go to-day;' and as Laurence's word was law with his mother and sister, the carriage was remanded.

'Where is my father, Timmins?' said Laurence, two days after his interview with Hugh Darville.

'In the small room at the end of the passage, next to the small drawing-room, sir.'

'Is he alone?'

'I rather think he is, sir;' and Mr. Timmins,

on whom very old Madeira was beginning to tell, hobbled out of the breakfast-room.

Laurence Bradfield had taken two days to make up his mind, and went in search of his father.

He was not alone—he was with his bailiff.

'Is that you, Laurence? Wait a bit—sit down, that's a good fellow. I've something particular to tell you.'

In the meantime he went on ordering new buildings for one tenant, whitewash for another, a roof for a third, a pigstye for a fourth: 'and so you think we may give up that bit of ground to Mrs. Wiggins?'

'Well, sir, 'deed I do. She's an industrious body wi' them two boys o' hern to keep, and it 'ud be a help to her.'

'Then let it be done at once, ready for summer-planting;' and the astonishment depicted on the bailiff's countenance was not more extraordinary than the apparent generosity, and glow of cheerfulness, which exhibited itself on that of Abel Bradfield.

'Now, Laurence,' said he, turning round as his man of business left the room, 'I've some news for you, capital news, extraordinary news, but you'll never guess.'

'I've some for you, sir,' said Laurence, with however less exhilaration.

'Well, well, that will keep. What do you think of a letter from Lord Mentmore?'

'I too have a letter from Lord Mentmore,' replied he, but with a face that did not place the honour of that correspondence quite so high.

'A letter—yes—very likely; but you're so slow; you never do see anything. What do you say to a proposal—a proposal for our Nelly?'

'I'm sorry the answer does not rest with us, sir; the question is what Ellen will say to it.'

'Say to it! What should she say, man? She'll go out of her mind. Fancy, Laurence! Now will they say I don't know the world, and the value of money? My Ellen Countess of Mentmore!—Mistress of Silvermere!—and half-a-dozen places besides! I haven't told your mother yet. Luckily I put the letters in my pocket, and opened them here. Ha! ha! A fig for my Lady Carrington and her airs now!' and the successful manufacturer snapped his fingers with great glee and vulgarity. 'There, read that,' and he tossed over Lord Mentmore's letter to his son. 'My daughter, sir, will be the first woman in the county. It'll take down the pride of some of these precious aristocrats; and now you can go and pick and choose among the best of them.' Prosperity and good-humour had made Abel Bradfield more vulgar than heretofore.

Laurence Bradfield read Lord Mentmore's letter, of which he had not exactly a duplicate, but a retainer in the cause. It was precisely what might have been expected. Amongst other things it set forth that the laws of hospitality had prevented his pressing so delicate a subject personally upon his guest, but that his affection was the no less ardent, his attachment no less sincere. His letter to Laurence begged for his aid in presenting him before her in this light, with all those other valid reasons for acceptance, which, with fathers and brothers, a peer of the realm, with some sixty thousand a year, is not likely to want.

'She might have been a lucky woman, if—'

'Might have been? What the devil do you mean? She is a lucky woman, unless you're expecting one of the royal princes to propose for her. Don't I tell you it will be the making of us all. These infernal Carringtons will bow their heads when they hear of it; perhaps they had an inkling of it when they recommenced their intimacy. They were all here yesterday—the new member and all. I hear he wanted to see me.'

'I saw him instead, as you were away from home. But doesn't it occur to you, my dear father, that this luck might have fallen elsewhere, if the Carringtons, for instance, had had Sommerton instead of us?'

It was a curious speech, under the circumstances, and came out partly unawares. His father, however, was too much engrossed with his own plans to see anything but wealth, honour, Debrett, for his daughter and himself; a peerage, was it not possible for his son? and looking at Laurence with more affection than he had done since he was at school, he got up and wrung his hand warmly—

'Come, Laurence, I know I'm irritable, and have my faults like the rest of us, but this has delighted me. You don't see it in the same light.'

'Not exactly, I confess, sir; perhaps I know more of my sister's sentiments than you do. Perhaps she might not feel inclined to accept Lord Mentmore.'

'Not feel inclined?' and here Mr. Abel Bradfield broke into a laugh almost hysterical.—'Not feel inclined; and why not, pray?'

'She may not like him—at least may not love Lord Mentmore—'

'Do leave off talking such puling sentimentality as this. Not love him! Where did you ever see a woman who did not love sixty thousand a-year? I tell you, man, with her property they'll be among the richest nobility of England. It's a capital match for both of them. If she don't love him, she must learn to do so, or marry him first and love him afterwards; but I won't believe it. Send for the girl;' and Abel Bradfield, quite put out by the appearance of opposition, rang the bell, and desired that Miss Bradfield might be sent for.

'Stay, sir; before Ellen comes, let me discharge one part of my duty towards you both. You know that Stafford Carrington called here yesterday. Have you, perhaps, overlooked one of your letters this morning?'

'No.'

'Have you then no idea of the object of his visit?'

'None whatever; perhaps you can enlighten me—you seem behind the scenes.'

'He was here yesterday to propose for my sister's hand.' Abel Bradfield rose to his feet, with every sign of passion on his countenance.

'Stay, my dear father; hear it all. You think that Ellen or Carrington has deceived you. Nothing of the sort. Carrington's attachment has been of longer growth than we thought, and nothing but our unfortunate misunderstandings have prevented its proper exhibition. His aunt, Miss Carrington, knows of it; and since we have met so frequently, especially at Silvermere, he has found opportunities of declaring himself. He was here yesterday to see you, to endeavour to conquer your prejudices, and gain your consent, as he has the affection of your daughter.'

'Do you mean to tell me,' and Abel Bradfield hissed out with frightful emphasis each separate word, 'that my daughter has dared to encourage the attentions of a man who is my enemy, the enemy of our house—whose family have treated me with the grossest indignity—who has done all in his power to thwart me—and whose wretched jealousy has been the curse of my very existence? Do you mean to say you are come here to plead his cause yourself? Traitor to your party, as you are, can you stand in the presence, sir, of your own father, and tell him this?'

Mr. Bradfield had literally lost every particle of colour from ill-suppressed passion; his cheek and lips were bloodless.

'You know, sir, my sincere regard for Lord Mentmore; and you must know that I knew nothing of his proposal until this morning. I could not foresee it; and, although Ellen and I should regret to oppose your wishes, we cannot regard the Carringtons exactly in the same light as you do.'

'Fool! renegade! you have the virtues of the spaniel and the worm—you can fawn and bear the heel of the oppressor. You have counselled her to accept him.'

'On the contrary,' said the young man, looking down with a painful effort at composure, 'I have not counselled her at all—her acceptance of Stafford Carrington is impossible. Had I known what I now know, I might have saved her some pain.'

'Excuse me, Laurence, I was unjust. But this other marriage must go on—you will help me. No girlish prejudices must thwart our interests. She cannot marry Stafford Carrington, she must be Countess of Mentmore—she looks it all over.'

As he spoke the door opened, and, not to give the lie to his last assertion, she stood before them radiant with the freshness of morning beauty, and looking only as Englishwomen can look in the face of early day.

Abel Bradfield was swaying about between violent passion and the necessity of conciliating his son: his heart was still beating, his breath came short, and he had not recovered his colour. It was with difficulty he spoke at first to Ellen Bradfield; his voice shook and his hand trembled as he essayed to give her a chair. She dropped into it, and sat back, looking first at her brother, then at her father. She saw all was not right. After a little beating about the bush (Abel Bradfield never looked anyone in the face, excepting when his passion conquered his fear), he said to her,

'Ellen, you are a fortunate girl; I have to congratulate you on a conquest.'

The smile with which he said this was a sickly one; the one with which she received his congratulation and answered it was open, honest, and healthy.

'Ah! my dear, dear papa, then there is no trouble. I feared a little opposition, for prejudices are stubborn things; but I see Laurence has been my friend.'

Laurence looked down, for he divined the mistake she was making.

'We are playing at cross-purposes, Ellen: there were no prejudices to overcome. Read that.' Saying which, he handed her Lord Mentmore's letter, and folded his arms.

She read it deliberately, taking time to think. She guessed the storm, for she knew the precursors of it well—disappointed vanity and opposition. But it was best to trim the vessel at once.

'Generous; so like Lord Mentmore. How to make him feel the disappointment least?'

'You will do that by accepting him. It is true that I learn from Laurence that we have been honoured'—here he laughed ironically—'by an offer from another quarter, which of course, under the circumstances, is not to be thought of. An impoverished country gentleman, and an earl with sixty thousand a year: one must be refused at once—civilly, of course.'

Ellen Bradfield sat bolt upright. 'Civilly—more than civilly. Lord Mentmore has paid me a compliment that I never can have deserved.' The tears started in her eyes. 'For his sake, if he thinks I should make him happy, I regret it is one that I never can accept.'

'And what, Miss Bradfield, is the fortune you have marked out for yourself? if I may be so bold as to ask.'

'I have accepted, and am ready to return, the love of an honoured and honourable gentleman, well descended and of a position at least equal to my own, of a true and generous heart, of spotless reputation, and worthy the friendship of my brother. If he thinks not, let him say so.'

'And who is this spotless, well-descended gentleman whom you and your brother have selected without the consent of your family?' His voice trembled, he breathed with difficulty, and again a ghastly pallor overspread his face.

'Stafford Carrington.'

The morning sun streamed through the window, and lighted up her cheek and glossy hair with its golden beams. Her heightened colour gave a Pythoness-like grandeur to her stature, as she rose to her feet to confront the insolence that trembled on her father's lips.

'An upstart beggar, that would marry you for your thousands.' Ellen's lip quivered, and her eyes filled with tears, but she showed no signs of yielding. Her brother interposed. 'Silence, sir.'

Laurence looked down again. His manner was cold, and he had lost that *moqueur* spirit in which he was wont to treat serious subjects; but Ellen was not to be thus put down.

'Thousands, papa—yes; but surely that may be one reason why I may reject the wealth of Lord Mentmore, to bestow mine on one that never sought it, though he may be glad of it.'

'Listen to me, Ellen. I would rather you should follow my corpse from this door within one week, than that you should give your hand to Stafford Carrington. Thousands—your thousands, I said: I could blow them to the winds with one breath. You are no heiress. There exists a paper which robs you, God knows how! of all you have.' His voice grew more and more uncertain; twice he stopped, and put his hand upon his heart to still its flutterings. 'Where is it? I know not. There stands your brother—fall back upon him. I tell you, you are no longer the heiress, but the despised daughter of the manufacturer.' His face was livid, but he still stood erect. 'Marry Lord Mentmore, I tell you. Come,

come, Nelly—the Countess of Mentmore, with sixty thousand a year.'

'I do not pretend to understand you, papa; but it would be more honest to follow your corpse to the grave than to marry one man while my heart was in the possession of another. I cannot obey you. I respect, I esteem, but I cannot marry, Lord Mentmore.'

In the meantime Laurence Bradfield had approached his father. 'There should be no secrets between us, father. I have thwarted and irritated you many times, sometimes unintentionally. I cannot enter into your views always; but forgive me. What trials we have to bear, let us bear together: we have thousands of blessings, and cannot be without our trials. We three can share them; there's plenty of courage amongst us to do what is honest and right. Let us keep them from my mother: we have still thousands, and to spare. Poor Nelly!' and he went round, and put his arm round her waist and kissed her. 'Now, sir, let me tell you why she cannot marry

Stafford Carrington. I have the paper you are in search of, to restore to its rightful owner. There is the release.'

Abel Bradfield seized it with both hands, looked fixedly on it for a second or two, tore it in half, and was about to repeat it, when his son and daughter caught his arms. He looked at them kindly, affectionately; the papers fell from his grasp; he put a hand upon each of them; a spasm passed rapidly over his face; and he was a corpse.

CHAPTER XI.

AWKWARD DISCLOSURES.

'Good heart, what grace hast thou, thus to reprove
These hearts for loving?'—*Love's Lab. Lost.*

UNREGRETTED, excepting by his wife, his son, and his daughter, Abel Bradfield died and was buried: he was too wealthy and influential a man for his exit to be wholly unnoticed. There are, however, plenty to worship the rising sun, and in this instance the homage was well transferred.

The suddenness of the catastrophe was a sufficient excuse for some delay in replying to the important business mentioned in the last chapter; but it was felt that to Lord Mentmore a reply, as early as circumstances would permit, was due. Both he and Stafford Carrington were at no loss to conceive why the answers to both were not immediate.

The latter question, Laurence Bradfield took entirely upon himself. He wrote and told his friend so; and pointed out that his sister, at this moment, might well be excused from receiving anyone, even himself. He more than hinted that obstacles might arise. Stafford Carrington was fain to wait Laurence Bradfield's time. He made the interval as short as he could.

Ellen replied to Lord Mentmore herself. It was a singular effort, and one which caused her much regret. Not, indeed, that she was not to be Lady Mentmore—not that she was not to be the envied of all her acquaintance. She had no regret to bestow upon this, but that she must inflict pain upon so generous, and so delicate a lover. She desired to make him feel how much she esteemed him, how much she liked him, and how far short of his deserving such sentiments fell. But she knew she could do him no kindness in deceiving him, so she left none of those loopholes which disappointed men love to detect. Fortunately Mentmore understood her—appreciated her. Her refusal made him her friend for life.

I am a privileged acquaintance—to the world these things are a dead letter. Happily!—for just conceive the malignity of Lady Hardingstone, at her having had the chance; the bitter astonishment at her folly by Lady Elizabeth Derwentwater; the petty jealousy of dear Lady Mary Gwendolyn, who is a good-natured girl where her affections are concerned, and really took a fancy to Ellen Bradfield; and the mute surprise of Lady Carrington and Evelyn, until enlarged views shall have fully explained—and very reasonably explained—her rejection of such an offer.

A fortnight after the funeral, when Mrs. and Miss Bradfield were in Eaton Square, when the greater part of Sommerton Hall had been closed, when Laurence Bradfield was living in a couple of rooms, for the purpose of concluding his business with Mr. Hugh Darville, and when the parish was again reviving under the sanitary influence of Scarsdale, whose ministrations had lately been a little infringed upon, one leisure morning presented itself. The best use to which it could be put, appeared to the young squire, as the people were desirous of dubbing him, to be by a visit to Miss Philadelphia Carrington. The lady was not ignorant of the events that had taken place, and was not, therefore, very much surprised when Mr. Laurence Bradfield was announced. After the ordinary introduction of conversation upon such occasions, he said,—

'You know we have sustained a severe loss since we last met.'

'The loss of a parent, I presume, sir, may always be considered so.' This was not meant to be unkind, but Aunt Philly never flattered anyone. 'And so Mrs. and Miss Bradfield are gone to town?'

'The house is nearly shut up, Miss Carrington, and will be so entirely in another week, I hope.'

Bradfield spoke with some degree of *empressement.*

'I am sorry we are to lose you from the neighbourhood, sir.' This was equally true with the other. 'I hope not for long.'

'That must depend upon circumstances. It is more than probable, however, that I shall henceforth live in the North.' The old lady looked at him scrutinizingly. 'Miss Carrington, very extraordinary facts have lately come to my knowledge, and I am told you can throw some light on them.'

'I'll tell you, sir, how far I have penetrated the family secrets. You have honoured me by your confidence—you wish to marry my dear Evelyn. I'm glad of it; though I see certain obstacles in the way. They must be overcome. Then'—and the old lady counted upon her fingers—'my nephew has made an offer to Miss Bradfield. I'm not so glad of that, for she'll have a large fortune, and I don't like the idea of the Carrington estates being patched up by a marriage. However, that's their business. I love your sister, sir; she's very handsome, and, I think, very honest and good. My nephew—I mean Sir Michael—has very strong prejudices, and his wife, who is a good soul, has imbibed them. But I don't intend a life to be sacrificed to prejudices which, between ourselves, have had their day. And now what do you want to know?'

'I think I've heard that when the Sommerton property lapsed, there was some suspicion of the existence of a release.'

'There was so strong a suspicion that my nephew was advised to try the question—badly advised, as it turned out.'

'Not so badly, madam, as you seem to imagine. There was a release.'

'Do you mean to say, Mr. Bradfield, that there was a legal redemption of the property of Sommerton, which had been mortgaged by my eldest brother, Sir Reginald Carrington?'

'I do, Miss Carrington!'

'And how do you know that? for your father was not married at the time I speak of.'

'I know it, because I have seen it; in fact, because I have it;' and as he spoke he produced to the astonished old woman the two halves of the torn release, which he put together. She adjusted her glasses and examined both that and the other memorandum with great care.

'God is great, sir! And you found this in your father's house after his death?'

'Indeed I did not.' And Laurence blushed as he said it.

'I'm thankful for that. How did you become possessed of them?'

He related to her the poaching affray, with which the reader is already acquainted.

'And where do you suppose this Morton obtained them?'

'I have no certain knowledge as to that. I have set men to work, who will do their duty. In the meantime, will you tell me once more, precisely the circumstances of your eldest brother's death, Miss Carrington?'

'With pain.' And she related the circumstances, as we have already heard them.

'Then those men murdered Sir Reginald?'

'Scarcely that; he fired upon them, and,

according to the only evidence we could get, they struck him in self-defence. They meant to commit a robbery, not a murder. They would have been very properly hanged, sir, in those days; now, I suppose, they would suffer a year or two's inconvenience, and be out again, on leave, to commit new robberies or murders, as the case might be.'

'Was there a man of the name of Jackson concerned in it?'

'The postilion's name was Jackson. He was supposed to have been tampered with. It could never be proved; but he made no defence, and has never been heard of since the affair.'

'I beg your pardon. The Mortons have escaped us; one by death, the other by stratagem; but Jackson is in this country, and we know where and when to find him.'

'And now what are you going to do?'

'I am going to deliver these papers into Sir Michael's hands.'

'But they may be forgeries.'

'I think not; and shall act upon my convictions. That property belongs to your family, Miss Carrington; at least I shall offer no opposition to any steps that may be necessary for the establishment of the claim. Thank you for your hearing and assistance;' and here Laurence Bradfield rose to go; the old lady rose too.

'Laurence Bradfield, you're an honest man. In this world to be told so, is not so equivocal a compliment as it seems to be.' He took the old lady's hand, bent over it, and kissed it, and left the room without recurring to his own anxieties.

Sir Michael and Stafford were in the stables.

'What do you mean to do with your horses, Stafford?'

'I've taken six stalls at Tattersall's for the week before Ascot. They begin to look pretty well.'

'You had better have kept them. I thought you liked them; and good horses are dearer than they were in my day; they were always difficult enough to find, and now almost impossible.'

'The difficulty is to find the money, sir. However, I think they will sell pretty well, and I must go to Ireland with the produce. I wonder whether Bradfield means to sell the horse he rode in the run from Everton's osier bed?'

'Mr. Bradfield, Sir Michael,' said a servant, coming to the stable door, and presenting a card to the baronet.

'Mr. Bradfield,' repeated the old gentleman, 'are you sure he asked for me? Didn't he ask for Mr. Stafford?'

'No, sir, he said "Sir Michael," I'm sure.' Sir Michael prepared to go in, and desired the servant to show him into the library; the library in which a memorable scene had taken place some months before between the fathers, and of which the sons and daughters knew nothing.

It was impossible for even Sir Michael not to feel the distinction between the present and the late Mr. Bradfield. Manner, education, natural and acquired powers were all in favour of the son; even his politics. Sir Michael acknowledged it by the kindliness of his reception. He asked after Mrs. and Miss Bradfield. He contrasted his last interview with Abel Bradfield in that very room; and half regretted that the man whom he had rejected as a son-in-law should be such as he was.

'Sir Michael, I fear I may detain you some few minutes; but the business on which I am engaged is so important, that you will forgive it, when you know it.'

'No more poaching business, I hope, at present?' said the baronet, laughing good-humouredly; for he had heard all about the fighting, and was mightily entertained at the capture.

'Not exactly; but the results affect yourself, as I imagine, very materially.' He then told Sir Michael of the recovery of the release, and his own impression that it was a genuine document. It took some time to explain; and Sir

Michael Carrington was too much interested to comprehend at first the full value of the intelligence. Of course he asked a great many questions which it was impossible for Bradfield to answer; as to how Morton came by it? where it had been hidden for the last five-and-thirty years? was he legally entitled to it? and how could his solicitor best consult Mr. Bradfield's convenience in dealing with any claim he might think it his duty to renew?

Bradfield could tell him none of these things. But he told him that until that day he had been unable, from pressure of business consequent on his father's sudden death, and his uncertainty upon some minor points, to surrender to him the document in question.

'Now, Sir Michael, I do so with a regret that your family should have from accident on our part suffered so long and so grievously at our hands. I thank God, that I have been able to make the first action of my independence the restoration of a right.'

Sir Michael was not a man of fine sentiments, nor very refined feelings or language, but he was an English gentleman of very high caste, and the openness of the whole transaction, the avowal, and the manner and address of the speaker produced a most favourable impression in the baronet's mind.

'Is there nothing, nothing at all,—think well, Mr. Bradfield,—nothing for yourself that I can do to oblige you? to soften this—this—what shall I call it? disappointment?

Bradfield did think. It required not a second for consideration. He did know what would have repaid him for all. But he stopped, while the words were on his lips, and instead of indulging his own day-dream, he said, 'Yes, Sir Michael. You can, if need be, spare the memory of those who have gone before me.'

He thought the danger was over, and was proud of having surmounted it. Not so. The conversation took a new turn, and Sir Michael Carrington began to discuss some political questions of the day with the young man. Insensibly he found himself listening to him.

Then he felt interested in spite of himself, and entered upon dangerous ground; the hopes and anticipations of an able and ambitious man, the prospects and immediate intentions of a wealthy and influential one.

'My mother and sister are in town. I must go down to the North after the session, and put my affairs to rights. Business is not to my mind; and retirement from it will enable me to do a good turn to a cousin, who knows more of it than I. We shall probably winter in Rome.'

'And then I hope we shall hear of your settling in your own country; you young men of position have a duty to perform by your people, your tenantry, and no man can quite do the position justice without a helpmeet.'

It was an unlucky speech, but a perfectly guileless one.

'Had circumstances not been untoward, sir, I should have looked for one near home. I did not intend to touch upon a subject so closely connected with yourself; but I might have hoped that time would perhaps have conquered the natural prejudice, which, I understand, exists to such an alliance, and have sought the honour of Miss Carrington's hand.'

Sir Michael was less astonished than might have been supposed. He had been made aware to some extent of Stafford's infatuation for the daughter of his enemy, but regarded it as less serious than usual in such cases. He received the present intelligence coldly enough. 'Let us not discuss problematical conditions, Mr. Bradfield; some time hence we shall meet, I dare say. Time is an assuager of ills.'

'I am going to town shortly, and shall be glad to see your son before going. Is he at home, now?' This was said very abruptly.

'Then come out, Bradfield, and see the horses; I left him in the stable-yard when I came in;' the baronet had shaken off his little attack of frigidity, which he began to feel was unworthy of himself and unmerited by his neighbour.

'Will you have a stroll round the garden,

Bradfield?' Stafford Carrington had never proposed a walk round a garden before; but it was necessary to go somewhere, for he conjectured that this visit was to him, as it was in fact.

Bradfield was provokingly silent when they got into the garden, and then began about the apricots, and the beauty of the Whisteria when in bloom. Carrington, with more consistency, asked him whether he would like to sell the horse he rode from the ozier bed to Sommerton.

'Carrington, I am charged with a message from my sister to you. Forgive her, if it pains you.' Carrington looked surprised, almost offended, while Bradfield continued, 'The sudden death of my father, and some circumstances you have yet to learn from Sir Michael, make it imperative that—well! that we should proceed no further at present.'

'I might have been prepared for opposition from your father, but I could scarcely have expected it from you.'

'Ah! how little you comprehend me. There is no person, with one exception, whom I would so happily call my brother-in-law. You know your own father's prejudices?'

'I don't think they weigh with you.'

'They do, though. I've a foolish pride as well as he. I believe it stood in my way to-day. My sister was an heiress.'

'It did not prevent my proposing to her. I have too high an opinion of her.'

'She is not so to-day. She has nothing.'

'That should not prevent her accepting me. We shall not be rich, but I shall have enough for both.'

'Nevertheless, the thing is impossible at present. Will you take my answer, or shall my sister write? Say which it shall be.'

'I do not wish to be impertinent. May I hear from your sister? The change is sudden, and there should be something important to justify it.'

'You shall hear from her;' and he did hear, that both their situations were changed; that a proposal was always conditional; that she could have bestowed wealth upon him, but that the manufacturer's daughter could not accept it from him. That he had more to offer now, and she less, than when their relations were different. What children the best of us are! Pride, foolish pride, that invents a rod for its own back, and inflicts a double wound at every blow.

In a few days he knew it all. Hugh Darville had the pleasing task assigned him of relieving two patrons, the one of his money, the other of his anxieties.

But it was later that they knew how the brother had toiled to dispossess himself of his money, and his sister of a bridegroom; and how then they both went into exile.

CHAPTER XII.

THE TWO THOUSAND, AND HOW IT CAME OFF.

'No, by my word; a burly groom
He seems, who in the field or chase
A baron's train would nobly grace.'

Lady of the Lake.

A SHRILL whistle, and a prolonged scream, and a heavily laden train began to discharge its hundreds, almost thousands. It was the morning of the Two Thousand, a treat for the upper ten thousand, and the place in which they were set down was Newmarket. Fifty omnibuses were there, one hundred and fifty flys, and porters innumerable in attendance. Mysterious men were about, and they caught still more mysterious men by the button-hole, and they all sought a corner apart. They needed not to have troubled themselves, for everyone was bent upon business of his own. Whence came they all? What singular combination of mutual intelligence made them all go to the same tradesman for their boots and trowsers? How did they get into these former and how did they ever remain in these latter? Ah! I know; in some cases it was the straps. As to the trowsers? Man is a fatty substance. He was boiled down and poured in a melting state into them.

The omnibuses and flys rattled into the one clean countryfied street, and nearly disposed of the little boys, newspaper vendors, and card sellers. They are honester than the card-sharpers who came down. And then they deposited their loads at the Duke of ——'s, Lord ——'s, and Mr. ——'s, and some went to their solitary bedroom to refit. Mr. Tattersall was selling young ones in front of the rooms; they were lame and weedy—they had been tried half-a-mile, and found wanting; they were too bad even for that. The ring was loud too, and very vicious. America and France were silent, grave, unsympathetic. And some of the horses were considerably knocked about, on that sunshiny forenoon.

Lord Mentmore had arrived the Monday before, in time for dinner. He had transacted business at Tattersall's that morning much to his satisfaction. For he found Stonehenge gone down a little, but a monkey restored him again. Still the horse was under a cloud.

All our friends at Mentmore's, or nearly so, we have met before. Wilfred Jones was there of course. Stafford Carrington too. Trumps and his colonel. Lord Dallington, Stapleton, and others. They had plenty of money on it, generally on Stonehenge, with perhaps a cock-boat. The lucky ones had hedged, but they had been let into the secret early. The Duc de Belle Alliance had on a pony and stood it all; whilst the Duke of Splinterbars having heard a whisper that the trainer's money was the other way, hedged immediately and stood to win a thousand to nothing instead of seven thousand to one. How the duke heard the whisper nobody knows. It was not from its being a loud one; perhaps it was, like some curses, deeper than loud. The duke, however, was not the only one who had heard it.

'You are sure of your information, Mentmore?' inquired Wilfred Jones, the night before, when Carrington and the rest of the guests were supposed to have retired for the night. Some were smoking, and the rest looking over their books in their rooms.

'As certain as a man can be on such a subject. In fact I'll tell you who my informant is, if you like; Laurence Bradfield.'

'He doesn't know much about it, I should say.'

'That's the very reason I trust him; he has no interest to serve, and has not deceived himself nor me. Those clever fellows who know too much are the men to take care of. However, this time I mean to act upon it. If I'm wrong, I am the sufferer.'

'Mind the public, that's all,' said Wilfred Jones.

'I begin to think the public is rather a

mistake. The public is always touting and meddling; it never pays a farthing towards my trainer's bill; it always puts itself in the hole by some blunder, and then abuses the owners of horses. It has all the fun and pays none of the money; I don't quite care so much for the racing public myself. But I'll tell you how Bradfield got his information, if you like.'

'I am a little curious; as it's a serious business to go into.'

'A man of the name of Morton, who is known to have been a former pal of Jackson when in different circumstances, and who has been seen here about his house lately, has been what he calls in trouble—that means, in jail. He wanted assistance and sent for Jackson. Jackson refused all aid, and they had a violent quarrel. The natural consequence has been a split between the confederates; and as Morton conceives himself to be under some sort of obligation to Bradfield or his family, he has eased his conscience by telling Jackson's secret. It's rather a left-handed way of repaying it, as Laurence Bradfield never betted a shilling in his life.'

'You forgot to tell me the precise nature of the information; we shall be able to judge better by that than anything.'

'Did I? Well, my horse is to have a good three miles gallop early in the morning in private, besides an unnecessary, though public, sweat. The calculation is that no three-year old can stand that and win in the company he'll have to meet. If there is any accident about it, the boy who rides him, young Strongitharm, a nephew of Jackson's, is to make him safe before he gets to the hill, say about the bushes.'

'And what do you propose to do?'

'I've brought over my own man from Silvermere, Evans, who knows quite as much about the horse as Jackson, and who has never deceived me in his life. He has two policemen in plain clothes. Before daybreak the horse is to go out; he will be stopt at the stable-gate, by my orders; and from that moment Evans will not leave him. He will have very gentle exercise instead of his three miles and his sweat, and I think he can win. There will not be the slightest row, or suspicion of anything wrong. Jackson will continue the ostensible manager, and thinks himself quite safe with his jockey.'

'And how about the boy?'

'At the last moment he'll be changed—I've a boy quite as good, and ten times as honest; and I think we shall put Mr. Jackson's friends in the hole, as it will be too late to hedge a sixpence.'

'Upon my word, Mentmore, you deserve great credit for your prudence. Most men would have had a scandal.'

'A scandal does no good to anyone but the press. I shall get rid of Jackson; you must help me to win this Derby, if the horse continues right; and then I shall give it up.'

Wilfred Jones's face fell. This was an unexpected piece of prudence for which he was not prepared.

'Give it up! Why what the deuce can you do?'

'Go abroad for a year in the yacht: you can come too. And when I come back I shall take the hounds. Good night, old fellow. We had better both be up early. The horses will be out at eight.'

Wilfred Jones took his candle, and mused long on this change of purpose. He fell asleep, dreamed that Stonehenge was a hare, and was coming up the hill, hunted by the rest of the field, ridden by a monkey in Mentmore's colours. The hare first and the hounds nowhere. When he was wide awake he reflected, that this was part of the battle of life, and when one went down another came on. If Mentmore was tired of keeping horses for other people to make money by, there were plenty more ready and willing to stand in his shoes; and though a change could not well be for the better, there were still oysters for those who knew how to open them.

The account which Lord Mentmore had given to Wilfred Jones was substantially correct. Morton had been recaptured and taken to

Saxonby; so he sent for Jackson. The terms which the former desired to make for himself when his sentence (whatever it might be) should expire, appeared to the latter simply ridiculous. Jackson treated him *de haut en bas;* which the stronger and bolder ruffian, forgetting the vast difference between a great public robber of thousands and a petty villain of a house-breaker and poacher, resented. The quarrel grew; and though the vials of Morton's wrath were uncorked, his secret remained bottled up as close as ever. The devil threw Laurence Bradfield in his way, who, admiring a hardy ruffian, said a few kind words to him. The leaven of malice and wickedness sunk for a time, and sincerity and truth rose to the surface. So the mode and the measure of the robbery came out. Dan Morton, free, was a dangerous person to Mr. Jackson; so Mr. Jackson had made friends with him, told him the 'how' and the 'when,' and was for having him in to assist in watching the horse; but that fatal poaching business spoilt it all. Dan Morton, an incarcerated jail-bird, was nobody; who would listen to him, with his cock-and-bull stories? was not Jackson, Mr. Jackson, trainer to Lord Mentmore, unassailable, even by the mistake that he himself had committed.

An hour after the train came in, that is at half-past twelve, the little town was for moving on to the course. Tattersall's rostrum was down, the newspaper boys were plying their trade at the carriage and fly windows, and the cards-men were more numerous than ever. At the opposite side to that which we have seen, where lies the railway, and the lime-kilns, and the training-grounds, the population made its way to the race course. Hundreds on foot, thousands on horseback, many in carriages; one costermonger's cart, and Mr. Joseph Jones in a very bad buggy. The sun was bright; but the wind was easterly, and the dust flew in clouds. The demon of sore-throats presided over everything. But a race is a race at Newmarket, and not a pic-nic, so everybody went out to see it.

The race of the day had caused much speculation, much excitement. Lord Mentmore's horse had been shifty; not so firm as might be, notwithstanding his own book, and his repeated assurances that he should win. Commissions had been out against the horse; not in influential quarters, yet for money. And now as he cantered down to the ring, before the first race, he vowed it would win. The French party was clearly not to be trusted. Their tactics on a previous occasion had been such as to shake the faith of all men.

'What's to be done about the French filly?' inquired Lord Scapegrace of a professional handicapper, who was supposed to know something about the stable.

'I shouldn't back her, my lord, she won't win.'

'What do you think of the favourite, Filcher?'

'I think very well of him; but there's the American just come with a rush, as good a favourite as Lord Mentmore; he opened his mouth last night for the first time since last Goodwood meeting.'

The ring was very full indeed; and the minor races were almost disregarded, so anxious were men to get information about the favourites for the guineas.

'Rappahannoc is at five to one, the American says he's in earnest this time, my lord,' said a pork butcher, who had failed in Smithfield and paid one and threepence.

'I'll lay you five monkeys to one, then.'

'Done;' and out came the books.

'Now I'll do it again if you like, or my horse beats him for a place, for the other monkey, if you prefer it.'

'Now, I'd rather back you, my lord;' and off went this worthy to make himself safe.

As the time approached the noise became greater, but the whole wore the decorum of a cockpit in which game-birds fight to the last and die without a cry.

The numbers were up. Thirteen of them. The most remarkable, Stonehenge, Rappahannoc, and La Belle de la Saison; the rest lived upon their private trials, and the public had not trusted them with much.

'I shall back the mare; I want the odds about the Frenchman to a hundred,' said a young swell, gallopping into the ring at the last moment.

'Don't be such a fool. She's as good as boiled.'

'How the d—l do you know?'

'Because I'm on,' said his friend; 'come here, I'll tell you all about it.'

Just then the bell rang; the horses were seen to go down a little distance off, there was a general move, the ring broke up, carriages made off to take up a position near the foot of the hill, horses gallopped away to the rising ground opposite the stand, and the real amateurs planted themselves at about the bushes.

'We shall know how it goes here, John.'

'Yes; it's mostly over by the time they get here; that is to them as has brought their brains, as well as their eyes with 'em. Why! who's that on the favourite?'

'Strongitharm, to be sure.'

'No, no, it isn't, though; Lord bless me! I know who it is; what's his name? Lor! it's that boy as comes down from our country; down near Lowestoft there; Markham. Lord Mentmore's own boy. Capital rider; they do say. How proud his old mother will be, if he wins the guineas, to be sure.'

'Well! they got Strongitharm's name down, anyhow, on the board.'

'Ah! that don't signify: that's the boy—so I tell you.'

It appears that Lord Mentmore had been as good as his word, he had stopped the gallop and the sweat; and just three minutes before the race, he had divested Mr. Strongitharm of his cap and jacket, and put up a favourite boy of his own, who had ridden the horse in a trial or two, but who was too honest to be entrusted when a robbery was to be committed.

'They're off!' shouted the crowd; and for once the world told the truth. Down they came from the start, steadily and in a cluster, with the bright sun gleaming on their many colours, the wind whistling round them, and the dust rising in clouds as they passed. At the bushes you could have told that many were out of the race, but the winner was yet in abeyance. Stonehenge was not in front, Rappahannoc was on the near side, the French mare leading on the outside, further from the rails. 'The favourite's beat,' shouted the short-sighted and ignorant, the French mare wins. 'Rappahannoc,' shouted the American party, and those heavy bookmakers Messrs. Pickett and Fleeceall, who stood to win thirty thousand on her. They were at the bottom of the hill. 'Ultimist wins,' as that gallant outsider made his effort. 'Rappahannoc,' 'Ultimist,' the 'Belle's' beat, Stonehenge is beat; and Mr. Jackson looked up from where he stood, with a face blanched with fear and rage. He knew better. At that moment the boy who had been riding as steadily as if nothing depended on his performance, saw his opportunity; in two strides he quitted the ruck, of which he had been in the front rank; in three or four more he had passed the Belle; Ultimist died away when he was collared; and there remained nothing but the American to dispose of. Within fifty yards of the winning post, Lord Mentmore's horse caught him, Rappahannoc raced for one stride, and Stonehenge went in a winner by a good length, amid the delighted shouts of a discriminating populace.

Mr. Jackson scarcely waited for the completion of the race. From the moment his jockey had been displaced, he saw that nothing but one of those happy accidents which are common to racing could possibly save him. His suspicions were aroused by Lord Mentmore's orders and the appearance of Evans; but the change of jockeys put the seal upon his doubts. From that moment he watched with a mixture of terror and rage the horse which was to defeat all his hopes, and to make him a beggar.

In that one race were gone the savings of his dishonesty. But he had made up his mind what to do; his preparations were made with due care. His name would have figured among the defaulters—what of that?—he could afford it, if he got away. The horse was not stopped, when he essayed to go. At that moment a hand was laid on each shoulder, and the face, which he knew well, of Mr. Champion, the detective, begged to speak with him a moment. There was a fly ready, and no resisting the polite invitation.

The termination of the Two Thousand was so far satisfactory, that the honest men won their money, and the robbers had to pay. Mr. Jackson was too conscious of his own guilt, a hazy sense of general iniquity, to resist, even to ask where he was going, or for what he was wanted, so he sat passively enough till he was in the train. Being there with only his official attendants,—for the trains from Newmarket before the evening are very empty,—he learnt the necessity of his attendance about one

Dan Morton, who had escaped from Saxonby (Morton was very clever at this); but who was supposed to have been engaged in a highway robbery some years back. It was suggested that Mr. Jackson could throw some light upon it. The examination was to be a private one: of course, the witness need not convict himself. The witness knew that. Indeed he began to wonder how he got where he was; he ought to have declined. Where was the warrant? And the liberty of the subject? It was too late now; and in the course of the day he was with Hugh Darville, Laurence Bradfield, and Sir Michael Carrington, with closed doors.

And how was all this managed?

Simply enough. The only persons concerned were anxious themselves to hear the disclosures that could be made, and Hugh Darville had no difficulty in finding Mr. Jackson, *ci-devant* post-boy; since of the bush, Australia; and just now employed in the capacity of trainer to Lord Mentmore.

Jackson had a well-founded apprehension

that more was known of his antecedents than was desirable. This made him obedient. Hugh Darville's was a name well known to him; and better known than trusted by men of his character. After some preliminaries they opened the business to Mr. Jackson, and very soon reassured him. At this moment his mind was affected with a diversity of ills, which lessened the poignancy of any one of them. He was fully prepared to criminate anyone but himself, and he did so. The much injured man told his varnished tale.

'Well, gentlemen, I was post-boy and helper at the White Horse at Claygate, a good many years ago, certainly; I won't deny it.' And as two out of the three men must have been alive at the time, it was no great virtue to confess it.

'Not much posting on that road,' said Darville; there was but little more difference between these two than is made by education and circumstance.

'Well, not much; however, as you ask about that particular job—'

'What job?' and Darville looked for applause; the lawyer's blood was stirring in him.

'Oh! you know very well, gentlemen. I know what I'm here for. It's about that case of old Sir Reginald. You want to know everything, and I suppose you think I can tell you.' Mr. Jackson was in for it now, and tolerably reckless; so he went for a good stake.

'We know a good deal, Mr. Jackson. You seem inclined to make a bargain. Do you know you are in our power, *particeps criminis?* It's a case of highway robbery.' Jackson scarcely looked as abashed as Hugh Darville. Certainly not as grave as Laurence Bradfield.

'There'd be great difficulty in convicting me, I think, a poor post-boy;' and he looked down at his own prosperous-looking figure, and laughed. 'Old Morton's dead, he was one of 'em, and Dan Morton's got away again. They won't catch him, he's away. I know he's gone.'

Hugh Darville nodded his head at his companions; it was true, he had managed it last night. They did think that Jackson helped him to what he wanted, money and tools. We know better than that.

'Come, gentlemen, the information is worth something to you; money's nothing. Let me tell my own tale, and give me one thousand to see me out of the country.'

'D—d scoundrel,' said Sir Michael.

'Bless my soul, the man's mad,' said Darville, staggered at the amount.

'Let him have it,' said Bradfield, nodding slightly to Darville.

'Five hundred's a good deal of money,' said Darville, doubting, yet hoping.

'A thousand is twice as much,' rejoined Jackson; some nods and winks settled that he should see Darville by-and-by.

'Well, then, I took Sir Reginald in the carriage to Patcham; he spent the morning with old Mr. Bradfield, the old gentleman of all, and your father. I don't know what he did there, but we stayed late. Coming home we were stopped.'

'How many?'

'Two of 'em.'

'And you couldn't get away?' Jackson was silent; in a minute he resumed.

'The old man fired a shot. He was a gentleman, and turned out; but one of 'em, old Giles Morton, struck him, and stunned him. They took his purse, and they found some papers in the carriage.'

'How do you know?' said Bradfield.

'Because I saw them. It was all they wanted.'

'But it was dark; how came you to see them?'

'They brought them to the lamps to read, and then I saw what it was. It was a receipt for several thousand pounds, and a release for the mortgage on Sommerton.'

'You seem to have made an accurate survey, Mr. Jackson?'

'I've seen it since.'

'Where?'

'In the hands of Dan Morton, who stole it from Sommerton.' Laurence Bradfield had made up his mind to know the truth. The last assertion was not a pleasant one as far as he was concerned. But he bore it like a stoic.

'And you couldn't resist, nor ride forward, with two men?'

'Look ye, Mr. Darville; there was one hundred pounds and a free passage on one side, and a bullet on the other. I chose the former. Would that I had never come back.'

'Do you know where the papers went?'

'I do; they went to old Mr. Bradfield, and Giles Morton put them away in a secret drawer in a mantel-piece. We all went away together, and we all broke our promise by coming back again.'

'And where did your hundred pounds and free passage come from?' said Laurence Bradfield.

'Giles Morton gave it me; I asked no

questions, and I think you had better follow my example.'

There was no resisting the impudence of Mr. Jackson. Sir Michael Carrington stared and said, 'D— the fellow; should you know it again?'

'Indeed I should,' said he, very collectedly.

'Is that it, or like it?'

'It is it. I can swear to it; it has been torn in half since.'

The case was closed. 'Darville, you had better see him alone now;' and the two gentlemen rose to go.

'Sir Michael,' said the younger of the two as they went out, 'there's nothing more to be said; it is as I told you. Forgive me for the injustice we have done you these years; all will now be put straight. Thank God it is so. Remember your promise. We go from England in a fortnight.'

'Good-by, Bradfield. We shall meet again.' The old gentleman shook hands warmly with Laurence; but he did not trust himself to say any more. He thought of his daughter, and determined not to commit himself by needless cordiality.

After all, he was but the first gentleman of his family.

CHAPTER XIII.

AN INTERVAL, BENEFICIAL TO THE READER.

'Intervalla vides humanè commoda.'—Hor.: *Sat.*

Having cleared up the mystery which hung over the rising fortunes of the house of Bradfield, and soured the temper and embittered the days of its master, it might be supposed that all was over. The public can see nothing, however, in a novel without a marriage; and as nine-tenths of our readers are of the handsome sex, whose end is matrimony, I desire to gratify them at the expense of the ugly sex, who prostitute that institution too often as a means. First, however, as an act of public justice to all, I must turn off those of the *dramatis personæ* with whom we have travelled so far; and then we will look to the matrimonal finish, which can be got at by skipping this chapter. It will not be complimentary to me to do so, for I always take as much pains with the last page as with the first, and intend it to give the same satisfaction.

Lord Mentmore is in the East, after winning the Derby; and as this chapter occupies exactly one twelvemonth in point of time, we may leave him in the enjoyment, or retirement he has sought, until he appears amongst us again. He has left the turf; having become convinced that, although it has its duties and advantages to be pursued by English gentlemen, at a vast sacrifice of time, money, reputation, and dignity, no man ought to tie himself to it for life. He certainly did his share of the work allotted to him while he was connected with it.

Darville was not found out, and lives a happier man and a wiser one. When he next falls in with a secret, he will probably make a better use of it than of his last. Even now society would be very hard upon him, upon all of us; and it is a very merciful dispensation which exposes our weaknesses and vices alone to that all-seeing eye which knows how much there will be to pardon by seeing how much there is to condemn. A lawyer's is a life of temptation; all honour to those who stand.

Jackson was right. Dan Morton was not forthcoming after his second escape; and as Mr. Jackson was anxiously inquired for at Tattersall's on the Monday, and has been as anxiously looked for and with as little success for a great many Mondays since, let us hope that he has joined his friend Morton. There is no fear of their reappearance on the surface of society; they are safer than any convict of my acquaintance, and their ticket of leave is post-dated at a very considerable distance of time.

Job Fletcher is thinking of reformation in the Coppernails Penitentiary, with every prospect of success, as he will have Nanny to look after him instead of Dan Morton. He is just the subject for a good wife's attentions, and will probably repay them; his little trouble came just in time to save him; and he owes a debt of gratitude to the Chief Justice, for locking him up during his insanity at Government's expense.

These are the outsiders, and we have disposed of them according to custom. The remainder must have more than a passing notice.

The lawyers, in a friendly way, took possession of Sommerton; and having taken a little of the gilt off the gingerbread, presented it again in admirable condition for eating to Sir Michael Carrington. Everything was most satisfactorily settled, and Hugh Darville and his friends deserve immense credit for avoiding a scandal, which would have wounded more than one of our friends. The pictures, the library, the furniture, are gone up to town. The works remained, and the Baronet found himself with an improving property, which was paying cent. per cent. of its original value, by the energy and capital of—the—the—late mortgagee. Yes! it was decided that that was the proper way to put it. And so it was. No living soul had anything to reproach themselves with; and the world was none the wiser.

Lady Carrington took Sir Michael to town, he having given up his seat in order to enjoy the country; he forgot that his daughter's claims led him to the neighbourhood of Grosvenor Square. 'D— it, my lady,' said he, basking one afternoon at a Chiswick breakfast in the full blaze of a July sun, 'I might as well have been in the House.'

'You forget Evelyn, Michael; see, she's with the Duke of Splinterbars, a most amiable person and the best coachman in town.'

'So he might be, my dear, without setting the Thames on fire with his coachmanship,' rejoined Sir Michael.

Evelyn Carrington *was* with the duke; and the duke, who was a good-looking fellow, paid her marked attention. He was always dining in Grosvenor Square, riding with Carrington from twelve to two, of course not unfrequently with his sister. But he felt that he made no progress. Evelyn Carrington was too remarkable a girl not to have admirers; but she gave no encouragement to one over the other. Lady

Carrington wondered why Mentmore was not among them. He had won the Two Thousand and the Derby; there could be no want of money, and yet he was gone abroad. A violent passion for yachting indeed!

Evelyn had been a girl of exceedingly high spirits; fond of society, gaiety; buoyant beyond expression. Now, though she was cheerful enough in a quiet way she had lost her elasticity. She preferred home. Her mother was loth to admit that she was affected by any recollections of Bradfield; yet suspicions of it sometimes forced themselves upon her. She had taken a great fancy to Laurence Bradfield herself, and honestly admitted the possibility of his success with a girl so young as Evelyn. If it was so, absence did not remedy, but rather increase, the disease. 'She'll get over it very nicely,' is an aphorism which requires investigation.

One thing was very remarkable. Bradfield's name, somehow or other, had been constantly before them ever since his absence. They had been accustomed in the country to hear him spoken of as a first-rate man. In London they realized it. He had written a pamphlet which was on every table. His views seemed singularly striking, new, yet bearing strict examination. His party regretted his temporary absence from debate. Sir Michael, and Stafford, who both led club-lives, were full of his reputation. The former would have heard less, the latter would gladly have heard more.

It is very awkward, certainly, when a man whom you desire to be forgotten by your daughter will obtrude himself by his talents upon your notice and hers. The more so when a comparison with other men is favourable to your *bête noire*. This was just the case with Laurence Bradfield. He had positively been playing Sir Michael's game; been running away from the woman he loved, who knew somehow or other that he loved her, and who certainly had the strongest inclination to love him. London society is not made up of these strong affections, and therefore it is a pity that the representations of life as it is, should deal so largely in them; but they do exist sometimes, and become obstinate in a heated atmosphere too. It was the case with Evelyn Carrington; and altogether the London trial was felt to be something like a failure. So, having got through Ascot, Chiswick, 'The Huguenots,' 'Faust,' and Mr. Gye's bill of fare generally; having done the Crystal Palace, the Castle at Richmond, one drawing-room, a Buckingham Palace concert, a Queen's ball, Rotten Row, the dentist, any number of 'at homes' and a batch of morning concerts, some time before Goodwood, and before their term was up, the Carringtons packed themselves, their servants, their horses and carriages back again for Spring Vale, with the exception of the M.P. for ——shire.

That gentleman is also deserving of notice, for he, too, was in love; and he managed to feed his flame without the palatable food on which his sister was enabled to nourish hers. For of all the thousands in that huge metropolis, who worshipped her brother scarcely one would talk to him of Ellen Bradfield. A lisping guardsman swore she was 'wemarkably fwesh-looking,' and a heavy cavalry man with drooping moustache acknowledged that she was 'one of the finest fillies out, showed lots o' quality.' Stafford could have shot them both, but then shooting is over under those circumstances. He swallowed his wrath instead of his adversary's fire. He was one of those men who chew the cud, who ruminate when they feel deeply. He could have made no confident of his male friends; his mother and sister, he was persuaded, would never believe in his weakness; and as to Aunt Philly, she—and then he stopped short. The very woman to talk to; she was not sentimental, but she was very honest, and he knew he would get the truth; perhaps without comment, which made it all the more palatable.

One afternoon, when Stafford had been out with the cubs in the morning and found nothing to amuse him afterwards, he determined upon a visit to Aunt Philly.

'So, sir, you're come to see me once more? Your cousin Walter is a great deal more attentive than you.'

'Then his are professional visits; he comes to see that you are not wandering from the fold. The good shepherd looks after his sheep, aunt.'

'I'm a very tough old mutton, indeed; and as I'm past wandering, his visits are very disinterested. Now, I wonder whether yours is the same?'

'No, aunt, I want your advice.'

'I'd rather give you some money, Stafford,' said the old lady, fitting her teeth, however, into her mouth, which she did preparatory to exercising her tongue with the greater effect, barking and biting, if needful.

'Why?'

'Because you might take the one, I'm sure you don't intend to take the other.'

'I beg your pardon; I came for nothing else.'

'Then tell me first what is your father going to do with Sommerton now he has it?'

'Do you suspect him of any difficulty in getting through the rents?' and Stafford rather implied by his smile, that he could have plenty of assistance.

'No, sir; but the house, what's to be done with the house?'

'To tell you the truth, I think he's rather bored with that part of the affair. I suppose he could let it, if he furnished it, for the winter. There's a little shooting, and good stabling for eight or ten horses.'

'He could do better than that.'

'How?'

'Lend it to you; it's high time you were married, Stafford.' This was a very promising opening, more so than he could have expected.

'Do you know that's the very thing I wanted to talk to you about?'

'Bless the boy, what should an old woman of eighty know about such things? I thought you wanted some information about Lord Castlereagh and Roman Catholic emancipation, which you know Pitt really promised, and left us a bone of contention for O'Connell to throw down, and your friends to fight about. But come, out with it. I hope it's a good match.'

'Match? you're too fast, my dear aunt, by half. I want your advice.'

'Oh! then you shall have it, and welcome. I'm sure you'll take it. All persons do upon such matters as that. Lady Sarah? The duchess will be furious; she means her for Lord Litterdale.'

'No; nor Lady Mary Borodaile, nor Fanny Beauchamp.'

'Then it must be that pretty widow of poor Lord Charteris, who lives in that great lonely castle of hers, with all her money. But she's nobody, you know. Only a dean's daughter; and though deans and those sort of people are on a most respectable footing in society, they don't go for much in matrimony.'

Stafford couldn't help smiling, though he hardly knew whether the old lady was in earnest. 'You're a great stickler for blood, then, aunt?'

'Did you ever know a Carrington that was not? They never allowed anything but absolute necessity to indulge in a Lord Mayor's daughter, or something of that sort, when they were almost out at elbows; and that's not your case, now you've got that poor girl Bradfield's property.'

'Of course; I knew what you would say; one does not live in a hunting county for nothing; blood—blood—mere blood. To be sure, one ought to go for blood, if—if—' The old lady looked rather amused, but did not attempt to interfere with the eloquence of an M.P.

'If there wasn't quite as much to be got out of a puddle, is what you are going to say; and from which I utterly dissent.'

'Indeed I was not, aunt; to be sure, after a time, you know, the puddle settles, and clear water remains at the surface.'

'Yes, but clear water is not blood, and I don't know of any admixture of qualities which will make it so.'

'Heigh-ho! I knew you'd say so; the thing seems impossible to you. I shall have to do as I think right after all, without—well! I suppose if she had the beauty of Venus, the wealth of Crœsus, the temper of an angel, the talent of a Dacier, Miss Bradfield would—'

'Who? what's the boy talking about now, Miss Bradfield?'

'Yes, Aunt Philly, that "poor girl Bradfield" that you mentioned just this minute. Do you know I'm in love with her? I wish to marry her, and I've told her so; her brother has refused me, but she has not. Now, will you tell me what to do? I'm afraid it's all water.'

'You'd better have fallen in love with Lady Mary Borodaile, or Fanny Beauchamp, but being in love with Ellen Bradfield, you'd better marry her. That's my advice, and I think it's the first I ever gave you, which you are sure to follow.'

'And my father?'

'Is a terrible Tartar, and will swear a great deal at first; but I think he's to be managed.'

'And my mother?'

'Did she ever refuse you anything? Wait a little, and you'll have her calling upon you and your wife at Sommerton.'

'What will Evelyn think?'

'Ah! she'll be difficult to manage. You'd better leave that to me; and as you can't propose till next year, there will be time enough to talk about it to them. When you want to relieve your mind, come and talk to me.'

When Stafford Carrington was gone, the old lady rang the bell and ordered her bonnet and maid for a walk in the garden, saying to herself with a very cheerful chuckle, 'What a match-making old devil I am becoming in my old age.'

'Miss Evelyn, ma'am, is in the drawing-room,' said Mr. Nurse, throwing open the door to his mistress at the same moment.

'And what does Miss Evelyn want with me?' said the old lady, hobbling up to her great-niece and embracing her.

'Miss Evelyn wants advice, aunty,' replied the girl smiling, a little mournfully, for she was not very happy. The following was the state of the case.

Evelyn Carrington had returned to Spring Vale, certainly not cured of her predilections by her season in London. Instead of forgetting, she had rather dwelt upon the memory of Laurence Bradfield, and public rumour flattered her choice. It must be remembered that Bradfield had not been wholly discreet; and that he had only been prevented from making the girl an offer, by a knowledge of untoward circumstances, which restrained him. Evelyn Carrington's affections had not been engaged, unsought.

A crisis had arrived. Splinterbars had proposed.

'And you love him?' said the old lady, shrugging her shoulder, that is to say, the movable one. 'You love him?'

'Indeed I don't,' replied the other, shaking both shoulders. 'You know I don't, Aunt Philly.'

'Indeed, I know nothing about it. Then you'd better refuse him.'

'It's very easy to say that, but you don't know how difficult it is to do so. You know what a splendid match it is; and—'

'Nothing is splendid that is not honest,' chimed in Aunt Philly, unheeded.

'And mamma and papa are so anxious about it; and though Stafford says nothing, of course he would be all against me.'

'And with all this you don't love the duke?'

'Don't talk of it, aunt; it makes my blood run cold.'

'Then you must not marry him, my love, that's certain. You must not marry anybody.'

'Not marry anybody?'

'Of course not. Make an excuse to get rid of Splinterbars. A most magnificent connection—a Plantagenet—almost as direct as Mentmore; and say that you will not marry.'

'That I will not marry—that is—not marry anyone, aunt?' Evelyn Carrington blushed;

but having come down to make a confession, she made up her mind to go through with it, *coûte qui coûte.* 'Must I say that?'

'Yes, my dear, if you have no better excuse.'

'I think I have another excuse; but how can I tell papa and mamma? besides, aunty dear, you will despise me for it. I love somebody else.' The last words came very slowly but distinctly from her; and she never looked up.

'My love, come and sit upon this footstool, and put your head in my lap; I'll tell you a story.' There was something very beautiful in this sympathy between youth and age. The thin, wrinkled face of dear Aunt Philly, bending over the lovely girl, whose eyes had filled with bashful tears, and which dared not look up to the place whence she expected aid. Aunt Philly began in a low voice, and it was wonderful how sweet it had become, and how memory softened the tones which betokened too often hardness and disappointment.

'I was not always what I am now, my child.

I am told that I was not ugly nor deformed. I think that is very likely true. I saw a great deal of society, and your great grandfather was proud of me, and made me his companion. In fact, he liked me better than my brothers, whose occupations took them from home. Among other things he wanted me to make a great match; I knew this, and tried hard to please him; but the right people would not propose. I couldn't help that, you know, Evelyn; none of us can. I could no more fall in love with the men who made love to me than you can with Splinterbars. It's a great pity, for he has excellent blood in his veins.'

'But I will try, dear Aunt Philly, if you particularly wish it.'

'It's not necessary, my dear. Amongst the men who came to my father's house then, was a captain in the navy, of the name of Gray, he was a distinguished officer, when there were more of them than now; but he was of the "aucune famille," as he himself acknowledged; and in our house it required a great deal of moral courage to acknowledge that. I knew how it would grieve my father if such a thing were contemplated as an engagement between Captain Gray and myself; you see, it was not necessary to marry anyone whom I did not love even to please my father; but I refused the man I did love, and who loved me. I bore it like an Indian at the stake, or rather like a shipwrecked sailor in sight of land, who refuses to be saved for the credit of his cloth. I refused poor Charley,' the old lady's eyes dropped all she had left of tears, 'and I never told my father, nor did he ever suspect that I had had an opportunity of doing so. I hope it is a noble nature that learns to bear well, without crying out. I tried it, and failed. I strove, if not for victory, for patient endurance. But it was too much for me. I endured torture upon torture; and all the diversions of my age, and the scenes through which I was hurried, served to increase my pain. I don't look it now, dear, do I? It's almost laughable to hear an old woman talk in this way;' and then the dear old lady put her shrivelled hand over the smooth brown hair and feverish cheek of her niece. 'My health suffered, and at last my father, I forget how, detected my secret. All was to go well. Had I only mentioned it before! said he. But I knew better, though he believed what he said to be true. Fancy, Evelyn, the pleasure of the letter which was to recall him from the dangers of his profession! It was written and sent. I lived in an ecstacy of enjoyment heightened by my previous self-control. The letter which I wrote crossed the one which announced his death, and brought one solitary lock of hair, as his last and only offering to the woman whom he loved so well. He was killed in action, and died as it became him; but I never forgave myself for the heroism with which I acted.' Aunt Philly stopped abruptly; at the close of a minute she laughed a little discordantly and said, 'Who would ever have thought of this little hunchbacked old woman with a lock of hair and a sentiment? I wonder what Mr. Nurse would say if I told him that?

Come, Evelyn, you must laugh, or I shall tell you no more of my personal adventures.' But Evelyn was past laughing, and only looked up in the little old woman's face, till she could see nothing for her tears.

'Now I'm not going to have you sacrificed for a sentiment, my dear; so tell your father all about it.'

'*You* must do that, Aunt Philly.'

'And your mother; what's to be said to my Lady Carrington?'

'I'd rather tell papa than mamma; and as to Stafford, he'll never forgive me.'

'But you've never told me the name of the forbidden guest. Well! never mind. I'm glad it's not Laurence Bradfield. Stafford never would get over such a *mésalliance* as that.'

As she spoke, the old lady caught her grand-niece's beautiful face between her hands, and when she released it, it looked happier than it had done for some weeks.

CHAPTER XIV.

THE FINISH: A DEAD HEAT BETWEEN TWO, AND THE REST NOWHERE.

'The pleasure past supplies a copious theme
For many a thought, for many a happy dream.'—Pope.

From June to June, one year, seems a long time to look forward to, a very short time to look back upon. It took all that time to combat Sir Michael's prejudices, and to reconcile Lady Carrington to certain changes. Two of their own household were traitors, or became so; for whether Aunt Philly told, or whether they found out each other's secret, Evelyn and Stafford ended by concerting to betray the garrison, and open the gates to the enemy. They were assisted by a vigilant veteran outside of the walls. She cared very little for Walter Carrington's invectives; who, being a country parson and the representative of Christian forbearance and humility, was more violent than usual. She was more lenient to the obstinacy of her own nephew and his wife, who, after all, were the parties especially concerned.

'You seem to forget, aunt, the question of family altogether,' said that worthy divine.

'You don't seem to forget, Walter, that if those children do not marry, you will be heir to one of the finest properties in the county. You had much better marry yourself than find fault with others.'

This was a regular facer and doubly undeserved. The rector was not thinking of his own proximity to the title, indeed he was older than his cousin; and he was proverbially a non-marrying man. But the dread of such a suspicion kept him quiet.

It is said that according to military science the fall of any place is certain under particular conditions: as, the capability of the enemy to surround it; its consequent blockade; and the absence of any superior relieving force in the field. Now as the assailing party fulfilled these conditions, and as the assault was not only vigorous, but continuous, the garrison was prepared to surrender, somewhere about the beginning of the following summer. It was an understood thing, too, that they should go out with all the honours of war. So Sir Michael and my lady were prepared to yield.

I cannot say that it was done without a struggle; perhaps a harder one than some people suppose; for a favourite prejudice is hard to overcome. It must not be imagined that these people entered into discussions as your ordinary vulgar souls would do; even as Abel Bradfield, if he had only been alive, poor fellow! would have entered into a discussion upon the Mentmore proposal. It was understood, after six months' coldness on the part of Sir Michael and extraordinary kindness on the part of Lady Carrington, neither of which had any effect upon Stafford, that he was, in process of time, to have his own way. Luck is the great divinity worshipped by people of position, and luck was left to decide the question of 'when' and 'how.'

It is a much more agreeable method of doing business after all, when the business must be done.

'Well! Lady Carrington,' says the most intimate friend of the family, 'so Stafford is to marry that beautiful Miss Bradfield.'

'I suppose he will some day,' says Lady Carrington, not pretending to be amused by the conversation, but implying rather that a Carrington is a privileged person and can do as he likes. Of course Miss Carrington is at present 'out of the hunt,' Mr. Bradfield not having declared in form. But Evelyn has no mistrust, and the correspondence with Aunt Philly is a very appetising one; she retails what she likes of it, and keeps the hopes and the fears to herself.

London has become exceedingly warm, and Sir Michael again curses a house in Grosvenor Square, but is compelled to inhabit it, during the stipulated two months. It is but right that he should do so. Evelyn Carrington is going through the mill once more, but this season with renewed success. She is gay, intelligent, charming, full of spirits; she must have quite recovered from that 'Bradfield' attack, which had been surmised last season; nobody knew 'how' or 'why.' The young *attaché* to the Italian Embassy thinks he has a chance; he tries it and fails—most likely because the offer was made in broken English, which he speaks but imperfectly. That's his version of it. But two or three very desirable English *partis* offer themselves, and are gently rebuked; just kept at arms' length. The beauty is growing proud. That's what the men in the parks and at Tattersall's say, when they have time to think of such social questions.

It was the very height of the season. Monseigneur le Duc de Belle Alliance was bent on a fête that should eclipse all others that had been given. He had many materials for effecting his surprise: an excellent house, five miles from town; a lovely garden, rich in exotics, and all those natural flowers which make an English lawn, redolent of sweets, and burnished with colour, unequalled in the world. He had a library the most *recherché*, a gallery the most interesting, combining gems of Continental art and genius, with the best productions of our own. He had wit, cheerfulness, generosity, unbounded means, and the very best confectioners in Europe at his command. Could he fail to attract the whole of London to enjoy themselves at his villa, from five P.M. till midnight, at the beginning of July? Certainly not.

The 'Morning Post' and the 'Court Journal' gave the names of the most aristocratic of the company, and added three or four, &c., &c., &c.'s, for the Smiths, Joneses, and Robinsons who necessarily now-a-days adorn a royal fête. You see everybody goes to court, and a person who has been admitted at the court of his own sovereign, is fit company for anybody. There's an especial exception made in the case of returned convicts.

So down they came to the duc's villa, stirring up clouds of dust, along the Kensington Road, obstructing the public ways, and frightening the Bayswater sparrows, about tea-time, who were not at all prepared for this sort of thing so far out of town, and so early in the day. Carriages of all sorts were there, from the most brilliantly-appointed equipages, with silk-stockinged and well-powdered footmen and coachmen, to the more humble conveyances of the non-resident foreigners. There were the neat dark coloured broughams with their quick-stepping cobs, drags with their loads of guardsmen and foreign-office *attachés*, the Lord Mayor's coach, and the sheriffs, with stout thirsty-looking women, all smiles, feathers, and colour. There were the loveliest women that England, land of beauty, can produce, from the middle-aged leaders of *ton* to the budding blossoms of a first season. There were the ambassadors and their wives, with their white or olive faces and bright eyes, and foreign-looking toilettes, adding a piquancy to beauty not altogether English in its quality or character. And single horses with cabriolets and broughams brought down the 'swells,' who were pretending an admiration for their countrywomen, which usually terminated in their own boots.

There was one carriage, bearing a freight not often seen, of late, in the gay world. Since Abel Bradfield's death, his family had remained abroad, and since their return to England had been but little in society. Amidst the towering structures, Ossa, Pelion, and Olympus all on the top of one head, was an unpretending toilette of the very best taste, in slight mourning, surmounting the loveliest face of them all. Madame la Duchesse de Belle Alliance declared her to be French, too well dressed for any Englishwoman; and Monseigneur the Duc vowed she was English, as she was far too beautiful to be anything else. In fact, he knew her at once; it was the daughter of his host of the preceding year. Ellen Bradfield was again in England.

Among the pleasures of the fête was one

which had been announced as forming a part of the business of the day. A lottery, the proceeds of which were to go to the distressed foreigners resident in this country, was to be superintended by the members present of the Royal Family of any country, or by their representatives, the aforesaid ambassadresses. Along one side of the lawn, forming a green alley, decorated with all that wealth or elegance could devise, the marquees of the ladies who turned Fortune's wheel, this time away from themselves into a worthy channel, were erected. Over each was the heraldic device and escutcheon of the family and country, with the name of the presiding deity at length. The beauty and gaiety of the flowers, flags, and embroidery were enhanced by the charms of the occupants of the marquees, where the dark pale cheek and long soft eyes of Spain, contrasted with the beautiful fair cheek and laughter-loving dimples of our own country, and the grace and vivacity of France with the finely-developed form and graver beauty of

Vienna or Berlin. Music and flowers were there in abundance; and here and there tents devoted to light refreshments and confectionery antecedent to the heavier hospitality which was to crown the day's enjoyment. The duchess's fête, like everything which she did, was unique of its kind.

Need I say that the *allée verte* was the centre of attraction? that as the men all went there, the women followed (of course this book is written by a horrid man); or put it rather, mutual attraction brought them there together. Need I add that when once there they would not budge? The good-natured duc requested the ladies who had drawn to move on; the equally good-natured and charming duchesse did the same by the men. Not a bit of it, in their admiration for themselves and for one another they would stand there to see and to be seen. In the midst of this terrific squeeze, which was alone unprovided for by an *affiche*, 'This way In,' and 'This way Out,' the language of all nations was going on, as each exhibited his or her prize. 'Beautiful,' 'Real Sèvres, I declare.' 'What! gingerbread? what are you going to do with it?' 'Make Charlie carry it.' 'What a lovely piece of point to be sure, Clara;' 'Ah! Lady Ellington;' 'Charmingly painted;' 'Doesn't Madame von Schönstein look well? slightest possible cast in the eye, but what a skin!' 'Is that the Austrian or Prussian coat?' 'There's a bonnet,' 'What a love!' 'What did you get, Lady Mary?' 'A small Skye, what did you?' 'A turquoise brooch;' 'Let's change;' 'Certainly if you wish it;' 'What shall I do with the terrier?' 'Put him in the boot of the drag;' 'Who's that, Mr. Carrington? do tell me, you know everybody;' 'Mrs. Noseworthy, of Noseworthy;' 'Lovely woman;' 'Glad you think so; you're the most charitable woman alive.' 'Dear me, that stupid woman has sent me out without a handkerchief.' 'Here, my dear, I've just drawn this; don't lose it, the lace is very good;' and so it went on, in English, French, and German

It so happened that at this time the crowd being very great, Stafford Carrington had with difficulty made his way to the neighbourhood of Mrs. Noseworthy, who was a very good woman, but no beauty, being large, coarse, red and loud, when once more the pressure compelled him to stop. He did so in front of Madame von Schönstein, and was lost in admiration of her very white skin, and that very slight cast in her vixenish-looking eyes, when he heard his own name mentioned almost in a whisper. He turned suddenly round, and there he saw for the first time since her father's death, Ellen Bradfield. She stood slightly in advance of her mother and Laurence Bradfield. To say that there was no awkwardness in their salutation would be untrue, but the inconvenience of the situation was overbalanced by the real pleasure of the meeting, and violent emotion is not fitted for ducal gardens or good society.

After the first greetings were over, the men fell into their ordinary habits of conversation;

something was to be said about the hounds, the studs, the house, yachting, and the clubs, the men who had disappeared, and the new-comers in the county since last season. The ladies were not long in entering upon Páris fashions, scandals, and Long Champs, in return for London, the new tenor, Rotten Row, and the fulness of Ascot. Sir Michael was not there, Stafford being enlisted because there was no house.

'Stafford, will you go with us to call upon the Bradfields?' said Lady Carrington, a few days later in the season.

'I don't think I can to-day, mother.'

'Why not? I think we ought to call upon them, under all the circumstances.'

'So do I; but I was there yesterday.'

'Yesterday! were you? and whom did you see? Laurence Bradfield?'

'No; I saw Miss Bradfield.'

'And her mother, I suppose.' Lady Carrington was pumping; indeed, giving herself unnecessary exercise in that way.

'Her mother was out of town, with some friend at Twickenham, and not coming home till the evening. Bradfield was down at the House.'

'And what in the world did you talk about?'

'Indifferent things, my dear mother. Amongst others, I asked her to be my wife.'

'Stafford, you're mad; what do you mean to live upon? what will your father say?' And Lady Carrington did not *pretend* astonishment at the very rapid movements of her son.

'Most likely what his father said, when he applied for permission to marry you.' Stafford had been a little spoilt since Eton.

'And what in the world was that?' said she, looking up, and laughing in spite of the serious nature of the news he had told her.

'Ah! that of course I can't tell; but it's quite clear what my father *did*, with or without his permission, he married you; and I don't think he has ever regretted the day, my dear mother. I shall most probably follow his excellent example. There, don't look grave, mother dear, I know you mean to give way some day or other. Aunt Philly has made it all right with Sir Michael; what Walter would call "squared the governor." But I can't go with you, because I have only just sent a letter to Mrs. Bradfield. I think you had better postpone your visit till to-morrow:' and she did so.

Everybody knows the steps by which these natural conclusions of happy novels are arrived at in polite society. How little shedding of tears, how little emotion externally, how well the anxious, doubting heart is taught to yield to circumstances; but it must not be imagined that if the refinements of life, and the demands of the world, polish the surface, so as to reflect only the objects which fall lightly upon it, the human heart has no depth. It has been taught to exhibit the surface as more readily appreciable; but it does occasionally happen that Cupid falls upon his legs, in the highest circles of fashion. Why that little god has legs as well as wings I cannot tell, unless it be emblematical of those slow-coaches, who walk into love with their eyes open, instead of falling or flying into its embraces by pure accident or from inconsiderate rashness. Love in a cottage would have exhibited a grand array of tears, swoonings, a heartless father, an unsympathizing mother. Love in a palace has such things; but keeps the exhibition of them only for the servants' apartments. Embryo duchesses do not drown themselves in the Regent's Canal.

There was a remonstrance at his precipitancy, when Sir Michael came to know all about it, just as there was a remonstrance in Charles I.'s reign, to which nobody paid any attention. Stafford Carrington, for reasons of his own, thought it right to speak out; and he did so. He thoroughly understood all the circumstances by which he had been thwarted, and the grounds on which he had been 'refused,' as Lady Carrington called it, until Stafford got out of temper. Then she called it so no more; but took the bride-elect by the hand, and rejoiced in her daughter-in-law.

'And where are you going to live, Stafford?' said Sir Michael, as he leant on his son's arm along Pall Mall and up St. James's Street, towards the end of the season.

'A small house in May Fair, sir, I conclude is the right thing with our income; we can come and see you at Spring Vale, if there's room in the Manor House, if not—'

'You'd better go to Sommerton. In fact, suppose you go to Sommerton altogether.'

'What! upon three thousand a year, sir?'

'D— three thousand a year, it's about twelve, it's only going back again. Poor girl! it would have been hers, if she'd had the good luck to have had no grandfather at all,' said the old gentleman, enigmatically.

I do not see how Sir Michael exactly made it out, for we all know that the reverse of that is the case; and that she has to thank her grandfather for the husband she has. It will all come right in the end.

'And here comes Laurence Bradfield.' He looked remarkably handsome; he had the same charming *insouciant* smile in his clear blue eyes and the same idle manner of walking, a heavy gigantic roll; but his figure had been set up since his absence, and his club habits had given him a *tournure* which he otherwise might not have possessed.'

'Where are you going for the autumn, Bradfield; that is, when the session is up?' inquired Sir Michael.

'To Scotland.'

'And afterwards?'

'I have no idea; perhaps to Ireland, to buy some horses.'

'Come to us; you know more about the partridges at Sommerton than we do; and Lady Carrington expects your mother and sister.'

'I'll come, Sir Michael; when shall it be?'

'Whenever you like.'

It is needless to add more to our story.

In the winter of that year, the Rev. Walter Carrington had a double duty to perform; and it is perhaps worthy of remark that one clergyman was considered sufficient to marry two couples without the intervention of bishop or dean. The house was full and the festivities were great; and the tenants of Spring Vale and Sommerton came in for their share of the good things. Aunt Philly did all but dance.

'Well, sir,' said Stafford, as he stepped into the carriage that was to take him to the rail for Paris, I hope you approve of your son-in-law.'

'I don't think a man of his weight, who can ride one horse from Everton's osier bed to Sommerton, at the pace we went, can be a very bad one.'

I've seen these two men since: Laurence

Bradfield and Stafford Carrington. It is difficult to say, in the race of life, *which is the winner*.

P.S.—Lord Mentmore has just arrived in London, he has been introduced to the belle of the season. She is the handsomest, best-bred, and wealthiest woman in town, a charming person mentally and physically; and he is perfectly satisfied that, having accepted him, she marries him for himself alone. Poetical justice required this termination. Had I not been able to state this as a fact, we should have had our publisher's box swamped with inquiries for his 'whereabout.' If it is any satisfaction to the fairer portion of our readers to know it, Scarsdale has the family living and is still unmarried. His cousin knew too well how to fall to kill himself, with hounds, but died of rheumatic fever caught by riding a quick twenty minutes in a waterproof coat, and taking it off afterwards. Aunt Philly, who survived him by a few years, when she heard of the death of the Reverend John Mucklestone, of Broomfield, Yorkshire, and her friend Scarsdale's nomination, declared her conviction that her nephew Walter was right for once in his life. John Mucklestone was what he had always asserted, 'a good one to go.'

THE END.

CPSIA information can be obtained
at www.ICGtesting.com
Printed in the USA
LVHW040024180422
716440LV00005B/441

9 783752 59556